The Adventures of Iris and Zach

The Adventures of Iris and Zach

I.L. Green

Bridge House

British Library Cataloguing in Publication Data
A Record of this Publication is available from the British Library

ISBN 978-1-914199-34-9

This edition published 2023 by Bridge House Publishing
Manchester, England

CONTENTS

Introduction

I felt empty just offering a gathering of short stories without preamble, so amble I shall. It must explain, first, what's in a name? Iris and Zach appear in many of my short works and later in a published novel. Iris represents the opportunity to overcome the symptoms of major depression/anxiety disorder accompanied by suicidal ideation, across all my works. Everything I write touches on mental illness and the accompanying struggle to stay alive, with the base message being to stop struggling. The inspirational source for the name Iris is derived from the American journalist Iris Chang whose promising life ended tragically and at a young age during a time in my emotional life when I was battling the same demons.

I rely heavily on transcendentalist philosophy to stay emotionally and spiritually healthy. This also shows in my writing. Thoreau taught us how misery accompanies all that is beautiful and wondrous in this world we find ourselves occupying. That one cannot be found without experiencing the other, and to eliminate either one leaves us void of both. Unfortunately, in trying to convey such forgotten philosophy, my writing may come across as focusing on the absurdities of life. My hope is the reader may find reason to smile at my focus and recognize each opportunity the characters use to live free, happy, and healthy lives.

Queen of Bavaria

"Queen of Bavaria?" Iris asked. "What happened to the Queen of Bavaria?"

"What?" I asked. I pretended to have no idea what she was talking about. My focus was on the half empty bottle of Chivas. When it came to whiskey I was a half empty kinda guy.

"You were obsessed with the Queen of Bavaria. Zach, are you listening to me?"

I poured another drink. I was listening, just not concentrating. Ice is all I could think about. Chivas needs ice. It's my usual drink.

"Ice?" I asked.

"It's in the kitchen," Iris said.

The kitchen wasn't one of my favorite rooms. It was dirty and messy. We generally kept the entire apartment in such a condition, but the kitchen had grease added to the grunge.

I had to hammer away at the big chunk of half melted re-frozen ice in the freezer bucket, so I could have the smaller chunks for my glass. I loved the cracking noise ice made as it broke apart from being dropped into warm whiskey. I was getting a little drunk. Iris was a bit high from a Tramadol and Valium cocktail.

I sat in the chair facing the sofa. It was covered with dirty clothes, and I assumed it was a pair of shoes digging into my ass. In my half drunken state, I didn't care to check.

"The whole time we were growing up all you ever wanted was the Queen of Bavaria. You saved money working at the Java Hut for a year. Looked into getting the proper permits for endangered birds, remember? Your mother wouldn't sign for it?"

"I remember something," I lied.

"Oh Jesus," Iris sighed. She stretched back on the

couch. Crossed her tiny dark legs, feet propped on the arm of the sofa. She wore only green boxers and a white t-shirt. Her tiny body resembled a preteen boy with its lack of the more pronounced female curvatures.

"Sometimes it seems like we lived two lives. When I was young and innocent, and then after Bobby."

"I know," I said. "It seems that way sometimes."

It seems that way all the time. Except for you, who seems to transcend, like you were unaffected. You have been consistent for the whole thing. Before and after. Like you know some great cosmic secret."

Iris reached for the pack of Benson and Hedges on the coffee table. She struck a match to lit the cigarette. Her face glowed orange for a moment. The tiny quarter moon slits which were the shape of her dark eyes concentrated on the flame lighting the end of the butt. Shadows flickered around her small pointed nose, and the base of her chin at the bottom of her oval-shaped face. She blew a big puff of smoke into the air above her head. I stood and reached pleadingly with my fingers. She gave me the cigarette she had just lit, pulled another from the paper package on the table, and started the entire process again. She smiled at me after blowing more smoke toward the ceiling.

"We were going to share the bird," I admitted to Iris. "We wanted a girl, but we had no name. A golden female conure of our own. We talked about it every day, like expecting parents."

"Remember," Iris said softly, wistfully. She was partially hidden by cigarette smoke across the room. I couldn't read her posture, or the expression on her face. "Remember when we thought my mother did it? She hated him so much."

"I don't think it was hate," I said.

"She beat him," Iris reminded.

"Sick for sure. I can't believe it was hate."

I was remembering summer lemonade, home cooked

dinners, late night snacks and music videos. The blue light of the television illuminating a dark room. Bobby moving to the music, smiling at me. His mother leaving the room satisfied our teenage high carbohydrate and fructose syrup needs were met.

"I still wonder…" Iris trailed off.

"Terminal burrowing behavior," I blurted.

"What?"

"It is how they determined the cause of death. Terminal burrowing behavior. It's the last act of a person dying of hypothermia. I doubt you want to hear about it."

Iris sat up. Took my glass from the table and gulped back a large drink. Her eyes were on me as she sat it back down. "I do. I want to know. When did you hear about this?"

I considered leaving. If I walked out now, Iris might forget we ever had this discussion. I could go and skip the whole damn thing. It never should have escaped my mouth. "Zach," Iris started with irritation. She would remember. This was Bobby after all.

"Suicide," I said. There, it was out there. Now it was going to be a long night. She stared at me with wide eyed anticipation. She took a breath, her chest expanding heavily.

"Terminal burrowers," I started, "are in the last moments before dying of exposure. Doctors observe the results; it's never actually been witnessed. The dead person is undressed, or partly undressed, and they have tried to hide somewhere. It's thought the skin feels extreme heat just before death. The clothes come off in a desperate attempt to stop the burning feeling. They hide from the heat like an animal in a cave, or burrowing into the ground. They are found behind trees, inside closets, the back seat of cars. If the exposure is heat or cold, the ending is always the same. Terminal burrowing…""That's how Bobby was found?" Iris asked in a whisper. Her eyes welled up, a single tear escaped and rolled down her left cheek. Her expression remained frozen in bewilderment.

"It wasn't some mysterious death Iris. They never did an autopsy, cause they knew. It wasn't an aneurism, or a drug overdose, or any of the things we thought about.

"I overheard the doctors discussing burrowers with your mother. He was hiding behind the tree by the lake. Found between the tree and the bushes, tunneled into a pile of frozen leaves, with only his shorts on.

"He went outside in the zero degree weather to sleep. I know this, 'cause he always told me he would go that way. He said he was free. And people who knew how they were going to die were free people. No one ever knew this. Except me, and now you."

We locked eyes, hers tearful. The implications of the story showing in her expression, framed by her long brown hair. It was like the day after Bobby was found. Why I picked this night, I have no clue. Maybe I wanted to test Iris. Maybe it just escaped from my mouth. Or it was just time for the truth. He was, after all, her little brother. Perhaps something inside of me could no longer stand to have this between us.

Her tears ran free, just like in the bright hospital hallway long ago. Her sobbing was so loud; I held her afraid the neighbors would call the police. I finally carried her to bed. Exhausted from crying and reliving Bobby's death all over again, she gave herself over to rest.

She slept; I stayed up. Looking out the window at the sunrise, I took a breath of the morning air, held it. Let the coolness of it sit inside of me. I exhaled over the dark city. My home rooted in the Midwestern prairie. As I expelled the last of the morning's breath, the yellow sun peeked over the horizon, like the shining wings of a regal bird. I breathed it in. The city was suddenly a magical place of youthful mystery. On the streets walked gods and goddesses. In the sky flew the wondrous Queen of Bavaria.

Like a slow motion scene from a big screen movie, the Queen gracefully beat her golden luminous wings against the wind, held aloft by magical radiant feathers. I dreamed she was someone else once. Someone like Bobby, who wanted to be beautiful; who knew how and when to die. To transform into the majestic being he longed to become.

Iris was awake when I went to bed. I saw her eyes blink in the shadows. The hint of longing on her face. It felt as though she was happy I had come into the room. We were still together. We were sleeping in the same bed. I was grateful.

"When I can't sleep at night," Iris started, "it's because I can't keep my mind off of Bobby."

"You have to have an invincibility suit to help you fall asleep."

"How about just you instead," she said as she pulled herself closer. I could feel her thin form against me. She rested her head on my chest. "Just give me thirty seconds."

"No really," I insisted. "When you are trying to drift off, instead of counting sheep, dream of having an invincibility suit. An energy suit which makes you invincible."

She moved her head a bit. Her eyes were closed. "Okay, tell me about the invincibility suit."

"You can't get shot. Or blown up. Or hit by a bus. Because the suit is invincible and protects you. It looks like a fancy space suit, but really it's just an energy field, so you can make it look any way you want. It's run by a little artificial intelligence devise which looks like a remote. You can talk to it if you want, and it will talk back. Mine is named Ingrid and has a girl's voice.

"With the suit on you can fly, go into outer space, or underwater. You can become invisible and walk through walls. So you can spy on people, or governments, or bad guys. Ingrid can also make a fazer blaster to go with the suit. It's big like a shotgun. Bigger. It's so powerful you could drop an airplane with it.

"And, if you desire, you can see Ingrid, or whoever your AI is. She can look like anyone you want her to look like. If you wanted your AI to look like Naomi Campbell, she would appear so. Same as the suit. She's just an energy field. It's like the holodeck on Star Trek."

"They didn't have a holodeck on Star Trek," Iris interrupted, softly monotone. "I've never heard of that episode."

"It was on *Next Generation*," I informed her.

"Oh, well excuse me," she chided.

"So you don't know what that's like. But they had rooms on Star Trek able to be programmed like a computer game. Same thing with the energy field. Except the invincibility suit is a little more complex. And it's mobile. A person actually could, if they worked with Ingrid on it, have an invincibility ship instead of a suit. Which would be handy, depending on the adventure. And the fazer cannon can be integrated into the ship. Which would be cool."

"This sounds too complicated to help me fall asleep," Iris said with a blasé voice.

"Well it's helped me fall asleep plenty of nights when I was having trouble."

"Naked girl Zach," Iris pointed out. "Naked girl right next to you. Don't need other stuff. Just naked girl."

"If it's so geeky then what's that make me?"

"Teddy Bear," Iris answered in a whisper.

"Well Bobby liked it," I said softly to myself. Iris never heard me. She slept the sound sleep of a weary mind, tired from grappling with the truth.

Previously published by *Foliate Oak Online Literary Magazine* 2007

Mixed Tape

Kira's favorite expression was "keep the change". She made good scratch delivering forty papers every morning, and every dollar went toward her goal of a new RCA portable MP3 player, at a cost of seventy-five dollars, of which she had saved thirty-five. When she saw the exact player strapped around a dead man's neck she found it hard to keep her breath.

At sunrise there was no one on the street. No cars, pedestrians, or other bicyclers. Kira's oversized newspaper bag hung down to the twelve year old's knees. She wasn't a tall girl, barely able to mount her bike. She had forgotten to wear her jeans this morning, and now the bag would rub her bare legs raw.

Blood was the first thing Kira noticed. The back window of an unfamiliar car parked in the school lot had been splashed with crimson. She had heard the pop while riding up the street. Like a muffled firecracker invading the early morning silence.

An antique pistol replica lay in the driver's lap. Blood and brains spattered on the rear window of the car. His head lay back on the driver's side seat, cocked toward the open window. Eyes open and lifeless. The MP3 player hung on a strap around his neck. Kira studied the scene. The man wasn't breathing. He had shot himself in the head. The entry wound was on the right side temple. A small hole she had to strain to see.

Kira used her two forefingers to close the man's eyes, grabbed him by his long dark hair and tilted his head up so she could remove the strap and retrieve the MP3 player. When the speaker buds were removed from the dead man's ears music could still be heard.

"Gin I Win"
Artists-Timesbold

Kira stared at him again, for a long time, the features of the man's face etching itself into her memory. Square jawed and unshaven. His long black hair fell around his neck. Over his closed eyes his thick dark brow relaxed in a final rest. He looked pleasant. She imagined he had a beautiful wife at home who was about to have a horrible day. Loving children who would spend the rest of their lives trying to make sense of this morning. Only minutes ago he had been breathing, listening to music, and for some reason he decided to put the gun to his head and pull the trigger. Kira considered this for a short time, while staring at the man's closed dead eyes. He could have picked that moment to have a cigarette, go for coffee and donuts. Almost anything, but he pulled the trigger instead. In an instant, everything he was disappeared.

Kira looked down at the MP3 player. A little blood dirtied the top of it. She figured out the stop button and stuffed it into her newspaper bag. Took one last look at the lifeless body, and turned to fold her papers for delivery.

Kira delivered her papers before returning to the scene of the crime at the corner of Fayette and Perry. By the time she did so police had surrounded the car occupied by the square-jawed dead man. Three squad cars were parked in the lot along with an ambulance and a station wagon displaying the title Coroner with large lettering on the back. A big man wearing a fedora was standing over the dead man on a stretcher. He hand rolled a cigarette and lit it, bent over the dead man's face, and with thumb and forefinger opened his eyes. He studied the eyes while puffing away on his cigarette. Then he closed the eyes, opened them again, and closed them before standing up.

He immediately noticed Kira watching from across the parking lot and took a thoughtful drag from the cigarette while studying her. Then he waved the paramedics on who proceeded to wheel the body into the back of the ambulance. Without his notice the small pouch of Uruz shag halfway lodged in the pocket of his jacket fell out and on to the pavement.

The detective felt a hunch the small girl knew something. She had been here this morning; maybe witnessed the suicide. But it was, after all, a suicide. Case closed as far as he was concerned. Why bother the frightened girl? She had probably seen enough for one day, or maybe a lifetime. He turned away and took a long drag from his cigarette as Kira rode by him on her bike, her eyes on him as she passed, music playing in her ears from her newly acquired MP3 player.

"Balcony"
Artists-Birdmonster

The cornflower blue princess phone was the coolest thing in Kira's room. She loved it and spent many hours on it. Talking to friends mostly. The phone was ringing at the moment, but Kira couldn't hear it. She had the MP3 player connected to the strap around her neck and the ear buds in her ears.

"Pylons"
Artists-ps

Kira's reflection in her makeup mirror caught her attention. She stopped for a minute and studied herself, the music blaring in her ears. Her long blonde hair was frazzled and in need of attention. The bags under her eyes were growing darker and becoming more pronounced. Her green eyes seemed to sink farther into their sockets every day.

She couldn't get to sleep like she once could. Sleep used to come so easily, but then she also used to be a more relaxed child. Feeling a bit melancholy, she sat on her bed and removed the ear buds. The phone was ringing.

"Party," announced a voice through the receiver. It was Vicky, her best friend.

"Where?" Kira asked.

"Where is at Cheryl's." Vicky answered. "When is now. How is on our bikes. Get a move on girl!"

Kira plugged the ear buds in and turned the music up to max. She stepped lightly down the stairs to the front door. Her stepfather lay passed out, drunk again, on the couch. The television was blaring, shining light blue in the living room. Her mother sat in the recliner watching reality TV. She noticed Kira and put a finger to her mouth for Kira to be silent. So, he was drunk and mean again. Mom wanted him to stay passed out until morning.

"Last Train"
Artists-Madison Strays

It was a surreal feeling, shuffling through the television light like a soldier behind enemy lines. The music being pumped into her head, a look of concern on her mother's face. Kira pointed to the door. Her mother answered by pointing to her watch, a signal to not be out too late. She slipped out and shut the door like a silent ninja warrior from an anime show.

As she walked to the garage to fetch her bike she felt in the front pocket of her jeans to make sure she had brought a double A battery. It was there. Her MP3 player would live for the night. She waited for the next song to start before peddling away to Vicky's place.

"Glass Souls"
Artists-The Benzos

"Jesus!" Vicky exclaimed. "You're just a party animal tonight."

"I'm not doing too bad," Kira said taking a swig of beer.

"You smoked from the bong, did three shots of Chivas, and now you're having a beer," Vicky pointed out.

"I should slow down maybe," Kira answered while giggling. She wasn't about to tell Vicky about the two Vicodin she had taken from the medicine cabinet in the bathroom.

"It's Sunday though," she said. She took another gulp of beer. "You know it was a good weekend when you wake up in the emergency room Sunday night."

"And are sick all the next day," Vicky said soberly.

"Nothing starts the week like adrenaline and a defibrillator."

"Are you just making up your own clichés?"

"Maybe I should be a writer," Kira answered, grinning from ear to ear.

"Clean up the material and you could be a comedian."

Kira silently mouthed "fuck you" to Vicky and put in her ear buds.

"Over and Over Again"
Artists-Clap Your Hands and Say Yeah

"How did you say you found it?" Vicky asked.

Kira couldn't hear her. The music was turned all the way up. She saw Vicky's mouth moving but couldn't read her lips. The Vicodin was kicking in and she was becoming very relaxed. She didn't care what Vicky was trying to say. She just wanted to listen to the music and drift away. The air was filled with the smell of smoke, booze, and sweaty teenagers. Suddenly one of the ear buds was removed from her head.

"I said!" Vicky shouted into Kira's exposed ear, making a face like she was trying to be heard across the Grand Canyon. "Where did you say you found this thing?" She pointed to the MP3 player strapped to Kira's neck.

"I just found it," Kira answered sluggishly. "Found it on the sidewalk while doing my route."

"Did you put music in it?"

"It was full of music. I've never changed it."

"Any good?" Vicky asked with an unsure look on her face.

"It's great," Kira answered. "I've never heard any of these songs. They don't play this stuff on Midwest radio, that's for sure." She pushed the button for the next song and handed the ear buds to Vicky who sat on the bombastic beanbag chair next to Kira.

"Under the Lights"
Artists-This Blue Holiday

Kira picked her purse up from the floor and dug through it until she found the package of Uruz Shag. She rolled a cigarette and lit it, taking a long satisfying drag, blowing the smoke up toward the ceiling. She enjoyed smoking and enjoyed being high. Getting stoned was her only release from torment, which she seemed to be feeling more often lately. Home was not a fun place to be. She was always on guard. It would be nice to be high at home, but she had to stay alert. Be ready at all times, or she would be blind-sided, by him.

Vicky placed the ear buds back into Kira's ears and took her purse from her lap without a word. The music was turned up to max. Somehow this made Kira feel safer, isolated from the social dynamic going on around her. She was happy to not be at home, but didn't really feel like playing the party game with the crowd.

"Falling Asleep in the Snow"
Artists-Auto Escape

The other kids at the party were dancing. To Kira's inebriated eyes it looked like slow motion tai chi. She couldn't hear the music they danced to, just the tune from the MP3 player. Her tight blue jeans were ripped at the knee. She had only one other pair. Her baggy t-shirt had a couple of stains on it. She had been wearing it a couple days, so it probably stank too. She hadn't fixed her hair or used makeup to hide the bags under her eyes. She wasn't planning to dance tonight. But she felt good, except a little nausea she knew would go away if she had another beer.

Cheryl was beautiful. She was thirteen and had the attention of the entire dance floor. She didn't go in for ameliorating herself like the other kids. Someone at sometime must have explained to her she didn't need to. She wore a simple yellow sundress and danced barefoot. Cheryl was as sweet as she was pretty, a combination often making Kira want to puke.

A pimply-faced artisan type of boy with red hair sat down on the beanbag chair next to Kira. His mouth began moving but Kira could hear no words because of the music playing in her ears. She turned to glance at Vicky who was concentrating on rolling a cigarette from some of Kira's shag and didn't notice the boy sharing the beanbag with them.

Kira removed the ear buds and was immediately accosted by loud disco music. She wanted to plug back into the MP3 player, or run for the front door, but the boy was still talking.

"… David Bowie," he said finishing some statement. Kira flashed him a quick polite smile and wished to tell him about the body odor forever adhered to her t-shirt.

"Don't you think?" he asked.

"Oh sure," Kira answered, nodding her head in agreement to whatever observations the boy had made about David Bowie.

"My name is Zach," he said holding out his hand. Kira reached out and shook it limply. Her cell phone rang.

Saved by the bell. She was in no state to be social. It was a text from her drunken stepfather. "Stay the fuck out of the house tonight," it read. He was in a tempestuous state again and didn't want Kira to interrupt whatever form of abuse he was performing on her mother. She started sobbing quietly, staring at the words on the phone. Slowly, she made her way out the front door, but not without Vicky and Cheryl noticing. Zach was left dumbfounded on the beanbag chair.

Outside, Kira had to change out the battery when the MP3 player died. She mounted her bike and road off into the night, ear buds in place and nowhere in particular to go.

"Weakness"
Artists-Morning Theft

Kira sat on the curb of Main Street by the Illinois River, crying into her knees. It was going to be another one of "those" weekends. If she went back home there would be hell to pay. It was cool out and she only had her dirty t-shirt to keep her warm. She shivered and cried, smoked a hand rolled cigarettes through the tears. Listened to one of the songs she had yet to hear on the MP3 player.

"Anchor"
Artists-Dutch Kills

With her eyes closed she could smell him. Feel his crude hairy skin. Hear his breathing. Kira hated closing her eyes because sometimes these thoughts would invade her psyche, and she would remember the times he had forced his way into her room. Beaten her mother into submission. Impelled Kira to take tranquilizers so she would be less afraid and easier to handle. Her choices were to take the pills or listen to her mother be beaten for the rest of the night.

Then, his mean dark eyes and bad breath, his putrid weight on her tiny body, smothering her. The tranquilizers blithely taking effect, easing her pain. Once more Kira and her mother would see the sunrise as long as she took the pills and closed her eyes like a good little girl.

"In The Belly"
Artists-Other Passengers

Kira's cell phone rang. She opened it and saw it was Vicky, pressed the talk button but said nothing.

"I hear you breathing," Vicky announced from her end. "Cheryl and I want to know where you are." They didn't have to ask what was wrong. They knew what it was and who had sent the text during the party.

"Now I hear you smoking."

Kira coughed from the cigarette smoke.

"And coughing."

"I'm downtown at the end of Main Street, the river end. Just follow Main and you'll find me."

"Stay there," Vicky ordered before hanging up.

Kira started rolling another cigarette, then decided to roll two; it would be a few minutes before they found her. She lit one of the smokes and plugged the buds back into her ears.

"Whitenote"
Artists-The Harlem Shakes

Vicky and Cheryl arrived on bicycles with a sweat jacket for Kira. She was grateful to put it on. The evening was getting cooler, compounding her foul mood. The kindness of her friends caused her to start crying. Vicky put an arm around her shoulder.

"I can't go home," she said to Vicky through the sobs.

"The party is over. I'm gonna stay at Cheryl's place."

"I'm worried about my mom," Kira declared. Her crying subsided. She wiped her moist eyes with the sleeve of the sweat jacket.

"We were afraid you would say that," Cheryl said. She stood holding her bike up, dark long hair lightly flowing in the breeze. "We're going with you."

He was sleeping in the recliner, in the dismal family room, the TV blaring and flooding the room with flashing lights from commercials. A half fifth of Jack Daniels sat on the end table next to him. His snoring was louder than the volume of the television. The entire house was dark. Kira assumed her mother was in her bedroom.

"What's his name?" Cheryl asked in normal speaking decimal, not worried about waking him.

"Jessie," Kira answered. She was in the kitchen looking for damage from a struggle in the dark. Vicky found some cold Spam pieces fried in a skillet on the stove. She helped herself to one of them, testing it with her tongue before taking a bite. The house smelled of stale dead air. The windows and shades had not been opened for days.

Kira did find her mother in her bedroom with the covers pulled up over her head. She saw the blanket rise and lower from breathing and snuck a peek underneath. Her mother looked intact. Face bruised and caked with dried blood. One eye swollen shut. Hopefully she didn't need to go to the hospital. Kira covered her mouth to stop a sob from escaping. Anger swept over her, like always. She wished he were gone. Wished her mother could find a way to get out, even if it meant sleeping in the car.

Kira suddenly wanted to get out and go back to Cheryl's. A slumber party would be nice right now. Her buzz was gone, but she was sure Cheryl's brother would have a pick me up available. He was a big druggy ever since returning from Iraq.

She returned to the front room to a surreal sight. Jessie was awake, and Cheryl was sitting on his knee. In the dark they were mere silhouettes. Vicky was in the kitchen silently waving her in. Kira slumped and snuck along the wall, not wanting to be seen by her stepfather.

Vicky was on her second slab of Spam. An empty vial with and eyedropper in it, and an empty pint of Everclear sat on the table in front of her. She leaned over to Kira's ear.

"He is really stoned," she whispered.

"What in the fuck is going on?" Kira asked in a soft whisper.

"Cheryl is really mad at him."

Kira watched wide-eyed at the dark figures in the other room. She recognized MTV music coming from the blaring television. Old tunes she was not familiar with. Cheryl would tip the bottle up like she was drinking, but her throat never moved. She just blew air up into the bottle. Then her stepfather would take a long drink. Kira couldn't tell the mood in the room since their faces were lost in the darkness.

Vicky munched silently on the Spam. Kira lifted the vial and smelled it. There was no odor. The bottle of Everclear smelled though. Kira's head snapped back from the strong smell of alcohol. She held up the vial and shook it for Vicky to see, who merely smiled with a mouth full of salty processed meat product.

"People Who Died"
Artists-Jim Carroll Band

Cheryl stood in front of Jessie and danced slowly, out of time, to the song from the television. Jessie didn't move except to take another long drink. She spun in the direction of Kira and Vicky, a dark voluptuous silhouette dancing like a pole dancer projected on a screen in a nightclub. But Cheryl was a child, with childish awkwardness; which didn't seem to faze Jessie one bit. He couldn't keep his eyes off her, and neither could Kira.

Cheryl was a year older than her friends, and a more filled out. She always was more developed than the other girls at school, with long shining dark hair, and a heart-melting smile. Kira could imagine the smile now, in the darkness, and what it was doing to her stepfather.

What was she trying to do? This could only end badly, but Jessie never moved, just kept drinking and watching Cheryl, her hair bouncing wildly around her head, the hem of her skirt swirling around her shapely hips. Enticing the thing in Jessie Kira hated so much. She managed to take her eyes off of Cheryl and fix them back to the table. Vicky had stopped eating and watched the dance with a serious expression. Kira's eyes rested on the vial on the table in front of her.

Jessie's eyes were glazed over. It was apparent he couldn't move. His attention was no longer on Cheryl. She picked up the remote from the arm of the chair and found the off button in the dark. Then leaned over Jessie, her hands supporting her on his shoulders. His jaw was gaped down, his eyes barely open, tears rolling down his cheeks. She leaned over more so her hair fell in his face, and whispered in his ear. "No one is allowed to make a guest at one of my parties cry."

Jessie's eyes closed and he passed out. Cheryl stood in front of him for the longest time in the dark, watching his chest rise and fall slowly as he breathed.

"Liquid Valium," Vicky whispered.

Kira figured out what was going on. She picked the bottle up and examined it as well as she could in the dark. Cheryl entered and confidently turned on the kitchen light.

"My brother smuggled it in when he came home from Iraq," Cheryl explained. Her face was pink and perspiring. She breathed a little heavy, but her eyes were calm. Kira held the vile up to the light so they could all see it. "Is it enough?" was all she asked.

"Probably not," Cheryl answered. "But this is." She held up a second empty vial.

Kira was sure her mother was still asleep. She turned the TV back on, and the three girls went out to their bikes.

"We won't get away with this," she announced as they rode down the street.

"Of course we will," Cheryl answered.

"We're just kids Kira," Vicky pointed out. "We wiped the bottles clean of prints and put them on the end table. It's a suicide. Who will know any different? Who the hell will care?"

"Which is why we will get away with it," Cheryl agreed. "Who the hell will care?"

"Your DNA is all over him," Kira pointed out.

"Bastard tried to rape me officer," Cheryl said. "Then he just fell over into the chair where you see him now. His DNA is all over me too. And I'm not showering tonight."

"This morning," Vicky corrected. The three were riding down the street into the sunrise. Behind them the full moon hung over the horizon glowing cotton candy pink. The morning was already warming, a hint of the higher temperatures in store for the day.

"Shit," Kira cursed. "My paper route. I need to go fold papers."

"Need help?" Vicky asked.

"I think you two helped enough," Kira said sternly.

"Stop worrying," Cheryl ordered.

"You sound like you've pulled this off before," Kira said.

Cheryl stopped her bike and gave Kira her famous smile. She winked at her and giggled. "Come back to my place when you're done."

"I don't have my bag," Kira said. "I'll have to make a bunch of trips back and forth."

"Don't go home," Vicky ordered.

"And keep your mouth shut," Cheryl added. She was still smiling. She glanced back at Kira then rode home with Vicky. Kira plugged herself back into the MP3 player.

"Trouble Every Day"
Artists-The Diggs

Kira folded her papers under the glare of the man in the fedora. He was parked in the same spot as the dead man from the morning before. When she finished with the papers Kira rolled a cigarette and lit it. The man in the fedora did the same. The assumption was easy enough to make about the man; he was a police detective. Her stepfather may have been found dead by now, or maybe he was still alive. Kira wasn't nervous but she was exhausted. At least if the police took her away she could get some sleep and not have to deliver the papers.

The detective puffed away on his cigarette studying her. Kira finished her papers and grabbed up an armful. She would have to come back for the others, as she didn't have her newspaper bag. She pedaled up the sidewalk steering with one hand, the square-jawed dead man's musical suicide notes playing in her ears, and her eyes on the man with the fedora the entire time. His gaze followed her as she passed by. When she was a block away he entered his car and drove away.

Kira didn't care about his presence this morning. She was running late and wanted to get back to Cheryl's. The cop wouldn't be there when she returned. She may never have to see him again, or her stepfather. She stopped to turn up the music, and then returned to her deliveries.

"Long Shadow"
Artists-Joe Strummer and the Mescaleros

Previously published by *Slice Literary* 2008

Presence

"I'm not at all unacquainted with sadness," she remarked. "You don't need to shelter me from the inevitable."

It was raining. I looked up to meet her eyes and my glasses became covered with water. The bill of her baseball cap was down to shield her face anyways. "I wouldn't try to hide the truth from you," I assured. The cold wind was blowing. Whether it was necessary or not, I felt I needed to speak loudly to be heard.

"Who said anything about truth?"

The bus was waiting. Now was no time for semantics: engine running, exhaust spewing smoke. The driver was reading something. He seemed unconcerned. I was getting soaked, and my heavy duffle was digging into my side.

"I was just saying," I started, "that I'll be back this way in the summer."

"No you won't," she insisted. She spoke loudly also. I wanted to see her eyes. Get an idea of what was behind such an allegation.

"What the hell do you want?"

The gray winter had been tenderly eventful. It felt like a lifetime since I'd been home. The future was one step away. The last few months would live on perpetually; the most glorious memories, fading into the warmest of dreams.

She stepped up, put her hands on my shoulders, and pulled me close. Warm steam escaped with our breath. I could feel her, alive in front of me. She leaned to my ear.

"Stay with me," she said softly, covertly.

That was unexpected. On an impulse I reached out for her waist, felt only the plastic slipperiness of her rain poncho. I knew she was underneath, soft and inviting. Behind the baseball cap and the rain gear was the woman I'd shared the past few months of my life with.

"Right this moment," I proclaimed. "Decide just like that?"

"All we have is this moment. There is no trip back this summer. The last three months are already gone. We can't keep them. There is just you and me, right now."

As usual, her thinking was going in different directions than mine. Her feet permanently planted on the ground. This would be the way of it then; she would be the anchor holding the string while I soared like an enormous kite caught in the breeze of time and space.

"I want red meat," I said.

"Negotiating…"

"And I'm tired of listening to Patti Smith."

"Blaspheme…" A smile grew on her face. Below the baseball cap, I knew her dark eyes were smiling too, sparkling with the shine of victory.

Over my shoulder she signaled for the bus driver to take off. I heard the transmission kick into gear. A wave of apprehension washed through me. Then it was gone, along with the bus.

"Nothing but you, me, and the rain," she stated. "You okay with that?"

"Too late now if I'm not," I chided. I turned to walk back inside the bus station. The duffle bag suddenly felt much lighter.

Previously published by *Birmingham Arts Journal* 2009

Dark Joy

"She's gone." The text message lit the screen of my cheap cell phone. What my best friend wrote pissed me off. She wasn't gone. Gone implies she can come back, which she can't do because she's dead. Shelly is dead. Just send a text saying she's dead. I know what Phil means by using the word gone, and maybe he wants to protect me from being found out, the same way he protects himself.

"Safe sex requires protection." Shelly once said. "A dead woman tells no stories."

I lean back on the sanitary Howard Johnson pillowcase and try relaxing on the rigid mattress. I close my eyes and take a drag from a cigarette. A luxury not allowed at home. The wife has a terrible struggle with the cigarette smoke I relish. She would also struggle with the knowledge of me diddling another woman. So would Phil's wife. A piece of seamy history now passed, dead with Shelly, just the way she wanted.

Dead Shelly now lying on a stainless steel trauma table at the hospital amidst the smell of sterilized air and unsightly green tiled walls. She hoped death would come during a nice meal, slowly being laid in a four-star hotel room, maybe in the hot tub. Expiring somewhere comfortable and idyllic. Her husband had other plans, as spouses often do. Hoping desperately to hold on to her, his happiness dying on the table as the trauma team heroically attempts to revive her from the heart failure that ultimately was her end. Her chest cracked open in an ugly manner that I was sure she would have been repulsed by.

Shelly was a voluptuous beauty. She lived close to that surface, cultivated it, used her looks to every advantage. She was vain, having her insides showing for the world to see would never have been acceptable.

"All I want to do is fuck," Shelly confided in me before

it came to this, her on the stainless steel slab and me running off to get drunk. "I don't want to lose my hair and shrivel up from chemo."

"It would be appreciated if you held on for a bit," I pleaded.

"It's my life and if I want to spend my remaining months fucking everyone I always wanted to fuck then it's my concern."

"What about me?" I asked.

"Consequence free sex," she replied. "Fucking a hot brunette your wife will know nothing about."

We held each other naked and she kissed me deeply. Wrapped her smooth long legs around my thighs to pull me in and hold me in place.

"Please be selfless tonight," she insisted in a sultry voice. "This is about me."

"But what about me?" I asked in a whisper. Shelly didn't hear me. She was breathing heavy with her eyes closed and her head tilting back. Her legs tightening around me, and a single tear trickling down her cheek.

And what about me? Hiding out alone in a hotel room far from home smoking cigarettes and casually emptying a bottle of Chivas.

"Character is determined by the hidden secrets of the soul," Shelly said softly as we held each other during post coitus reverie. "A part of me will inconspicuously influence every iterative aspect of your life from this night on. In this way, I'll always be your obscure dark joy."

She was wrong. I took a drag from my cigarette. "Iterative," I said angrily in the empty room. Must have been on her word of the day calendar.

Previously published by *Everyday Fiction* 2014

First World

a handful of pills won't ward off the icy steel
and pearls of blood spelling out the name
of the soul lost to unreciprocated imploring

my toes are cold and soul darkened
with the sickness of the first world
bourgeois early morning angst

iPod on replay, memorizing songs
keyboard stroked like the clavier of a piano
my fluency has no witness but the morning star

don't open the door
I want my soul to breathe free
while you wait in the hall
with all of your blond hair
blue eyes and straight heart

Ingrid sat in the driver's seat of her mother's Escalade and studied the blood on her hand. She didn't want to go to the hospital again, but knew that if she kept this up she would end up back in the emergency room being stitched up and listening to the doctor preach to her once again about acting out.

With her other hand she managed to open her phone and text Lisa again. "Where the hell are you?" she asked aloud to the emptiness of the SUV. The engine was still running. She set down the phone and plugged her iPod into the dash, tapped the screen until Zola Jesus appeared, turned up the volume so she could see the rearview mirror vibrate with the pounding of the drums and the steady rhythm of the bass guitar.

"Are you suicidal?" the doctor asked last time. She looked at her with bored tired eyes from a long shift and too much bullshit, and Ingrid, just more blood and bunkum. Another sixteen year old too bored to think of any other way to cure their tedium. "Are you going to hurt yourself or anyone else?"

What kind of question was that? Of course Ingrid was going to hurt herself. Why was she in the hospital in the first place? She felt the loose stitches on her thigh again. Her hand came away with more blood. Picking, picking, picking. Always picking and scratching. Digging with her nails until the blood came. She reached for her white towel, always a white towel. She loved the crimson on the white cloth. She pressed on the stitches with the towel, hoping to stop the bleeding before it ran all over the leather driver's seat.

Her phone vibrated. "I can get you about ten," read the text from Lisa.

"Please hurry," Ingrid replied. Ten Klonopin, she was already anticipating the relief. Her stomach was in knots, her chest tight, breathing was difficult. She looked into the vibrating mirror. Dark foreboding eyes stared back. She hated her dark eyes and dark hair. She kept it short so as to minimize the disgust she had for it. People told her she looked like Wynona Ryder, she envisioned Wednesday Adams instead.

Besides, Winona Ryder was actually a blond. Ingrid had read that on IMDB. Someone told her to cultivate a dark look, so for whatever reason, she did; dark hair, dark eyes, oval face with a pointed chin. She could slightly see the resemblance in the mirror. Way too skinny though, short with little boy legs. When she thought of her legs she remembered to maintain the pressure on her thigh. A car drove by and the headlights flashed inside of the Escalade. She noticed blood on her skirt.

“Shit,” Ingrid said aloud. The skirt would have to disappear. She didn’t know how to remove blood stains from her clothes and she couldn’t let her mother see it. Another car passed her. She was positioned in a dark corner of the Wal-Mart parking lot. She wondered what the hell would possess someone to drive their car out past the SUV. Did she look suspicious? Were people just curious?

Ingrid was going to go inside the store but felt the wetness still on her fingers. The store held her heart’s desire, carpet cutting blades, her favorite. She remembered the other kids in the psych ward saying that they frequented drug stores for shaving blades. She never admitted to her perusing the hardware section of Wal-Mart for her carpet cutter replacement blades, big, thick, extra sharp with a hole in them that she could string her gold chain through. Wear it under her blouse where no one could see. Fondle it at school while some teacher rambled on about math or economics.

It made her shiver to think about the touch of the cool sharpness against her skin. In so doing she had forgotten her anxiety, as if she had released a few of her endorphins just remembering, by merely anticipating. The bleeding had stopped where she had been picking at her stitches. Now Ingrid had to decide. Go inside or drive home. Deciding quickly, she turned the ignition and the car went silent. Zola Jesus stopped suddenly. Ingrid’s ear rang a bit. She knew how this would go; her sitting cross-legged on the tile of her bathroom floor, a blade in one hand and a white towel in the other. The big triangle shaped blade that she was now going to purchase inside of the store. She called it the fingernail of God.

The cashier didn’t bat an eye as he rang up Ingrid’s purchases. She was nervous about what the man at the register might think, so she found other items, hoping that the blade would go unnoticed among the collection of crap she was buying. Chocolate bars, blonde hair dye, a Red Bull, a freshly roasted butter and herb chicken, and a package of white kitchen towels. She wasn't really going to use the blonde hair dye, and she probably would throw away the chicken. The chocolate and Red Bull, though, would be consumed on the ride home.

The bathroom began to smell of copper as Ingrid opened the skin on her legs with the blade. Such was her mania, to cut, feel pain, experience release. The endorphins kicked in, she relaxed, yawned. Her eyes felt heavy. She could breathe. The red on the white cloth of the towel was like an abstract painting. Ingrid practiced expressionism, wiping blood and looking at the stains. It made her smile to see the patterns. The towel would have to disappear along with her blood stained clothes.

Ingrid cut herself above the hem of her skirt. It was summer after all, and she didn't want to wear jeans through the hot months ahead. Her arms were another matter. Long sleeves would have to be worn during school next semester. She didn't want anyone commenting on the red raw digs along her wrist and up her forearm. Her mother had not seen the new scars yet. That would be another matter to contend with. She didn't want to think about it yet. Maybe tomorrow she would wear a t-shirt and let Mother have at her. She was never happy with Ingrid's cuts, but she was getting used to them. Ingrid's only fear was being hospitalized again. Mother had admitted her numerous times, and after the ER visit, she just may do it again. Ingrid hated the psyche ward. She wasn't suicidal, just anxious, and no one had any answers for her.

The bleeding had stopped where the stitches were loosened. Ingrid silently berated herself for picking at them. She couldn't help herself though. And they itched. Once she started scratching, she would lose track of what she was doing, and the picking would begin until she noticed the blood flow. That scar would never heal.

The phone buzzed, Ingrid read the text. “I’m here.” It was Lisa.

“The door is open,” Ingrid texted back. She hastily mopped up the blood from the bathroom tile.

Lisa appeared at the bathroom door. She held a handful of little yellow pills toward Ingrid, who snatched them up greedily.

“Only take one,” Lisa ordered.

“Thanks,” Ingrid said.

“Are you cutting?”

“No,” Ingrid lied.

Lisa glared at Ingrid, trying to read her mood while she placed a pill in her mouth.

“Put it under your tongue and let it dissolve,” Lisa suggested.

Ingrid knew in a couple minutes she would feel euphoria. The knots in her stomach would unwind. Her breathing would come easier. She would not need to cut herself the rest of the night. In the dirty close hamper lay her blood stained white towel wrapped around the triangular shaped blade.

Lisa walked out of the bathroom and into the kitchen. She opened the refrigerator and helped herself to a diet cola. Lisa, wearing short shorts and showing off her perfectly tapered legs. Her long blonde hair was pulled back into a ponytail. Her blonde eyebrows and fair skin enhanced her bright blue eyes. Ingrid followed her, watched her every move. She slipped another Klonopin under her tongue while Lisa wasn’t looking.

“I’ve gotta go,” Lisa announced. “Meeting Kevin.”

“Kevin…” Ingrid repeated glumly.

“Are you okay?”

“I will be soon,” Ingrid quipped.

“You okay to be alone?”

“I think so.”

“You’ll call me if you’re not?”

“I might be a little lonely.”

“Do you want me to swing back by after I pick up Kevin?”

“No!” Ingrid answered with a bit too much passion.

Lisa walked over and hugged Ingrid, who held on for dear life. If only she would stay. If only they could have an old fashioned sleepover, just the two of them. Lisa pulled back and made for the front door.

“Don’t do anything stupid,” she said as she walked out.

The door shut behind Lisa displaying a large full length mirror attached to the back. Ingrid looked at her tiny frame, lifted her skirt to expose her left thigh. Carved into her skin with jagged sharp letters, was the name Lisa. Tiny beads of congealed blood had formed around the cuts. She dropped her skirt and walked slowly to her bedroom. She threw herself backwards onto her bed and remembered the clothes hamper. She promised herself she would clean up before her mother came home.

Ingrid slipped two more pills into her mouth. Sighed, and lamented to the ceiling. “Why do I always fall for the straight ones?”

Previously published by *Bluffs Literary Magazine* 2013

Eugene

"I've been up for about ten minutes," Juan said. Two guards stood outside of the bars of Eugene and Juan's cell. One of the guards was an older grey haired man, the other a much younger and overweight man. "I woke up and he was like that," Juan added.

"He was released from psych too early," the older guard said.

Eugene entered prison under a suicide watch and spent the first month of his incarceration on the eighth floor mental ward. He suffered from clinical depression, but he could be functional. It took him the entire month to persuade the psych ward staff that he was not going to hurt himself and he was ready to be put into general population.

"He shouldn't have been allowed to have access to shoe laces," said the fat guard.

In the back, by the window that looked out over the exercise yard, was a dark figure mostly hidden in the shadow of the corner. Beneath the darkness where a little light was showing, a pair of feet with white athletic socks could be seen suspended in the air as if Eugene was levitating inside of the cell. Outside the window lightning flashed. The sound of rain pouring onto the roof could be heard from just above.

Eugene was convicted on vehicular manslaughter charges and sentenced to life for killing a woman and her eight-year-old daughter. He was high on weed and had three beers, so he drove off. About ninety days later he was caught at a traffic stop where a warrant showed up under his name on the police database. The name Eugene flashed on the computer screen in the arresting officer's patrol car; manslaughter, leaving the scene of a crime, possible DUI.

"Looks like he tied himself off on the air vent," said the fat guard.

“Ten minutes you say?” asked the older guard.

“He twitches a little once in a while,” Juan stated in a matter of fact manner. “Sometimes one of his legs kicks.”

Juan was a young man facing ten years for meth transportation. It would have been a lesser sentence for a man who didn’t take half of the Phoenix police force on a wild car chase from the city streets to the high desert where his radiator overheated and the engine block cracked.

Juan was leaning his arms on the bars of his cell door. His dark eyes looked from the fat guard to the old guard. He met eyes with both of them. Keeping quiet even though he wanted to scream out about how creeped he was being in this room with this half dead man kicking in the dark.

Some specters leave the body well before the death of their host. Like a cold vapor escaping into the wind. One pass about the scene. Two prison guards outside of the cell. Juan waits patiently to be taken out. He doesn’t care where. They could put him out in the rain for all he cared. Just so he was out and away from Eugene. Another cold sweep around the group; the old man with the grey hair, he is afraid. It shows in his eyes.

Probably Juan and the fat guy saw this too. The fat guy, he just wanted to get out of there. And the cold vapor finally escapes into the storm.

When the lightning flashes it causes a strobe like effect in Juan and Eugene’s cell. A violent light invading the cell like pyro techniques during a rock concert; the light flashes across the bloated face of the hanging man. Eugene’s closed eyes could be seen during the flashes.

“Want me to report this?” the fat guard asked, his hand on the shortwave device attached at his belt.

“Shit,” the old guard said. “Don’t call it in yet,” he answered.

“Why not?”

"Cause he is probably still alive. If we open the cell we can tell for sure. Check for a pulse. If he is alive they will want us to cut Eugene down. I've seen this before."

"So…" prodded the fat guard.

"If he isn't dead yet, his brain is fucked for sure. He will live his life a vegetable on the medical ward. People bitch about the price of keeping inmates housed now. If only they knew the cost to keep a vegetable alive.

"Anyways, it wasn't an accident. He wanted to die. He basically strangled himself. The air has been cut off to the brain for at least ten minutes now."

The fat guard stayed his hand as he pondered this, his fingers rested on the shortwave attached to his belt, a quizzical look on his face.

"Besides, Juan here wants to get the hell out of that cell," the old guard explained. "Let's get him cuffed and out of there."

"He was a nice guy," Juan explained as they walked down the hallway to the holding cell. "Not much of a talker though."

The door to Juan and Eugene's cell stood open. The wind from the storm could be heard coming from the window. It was strong enough to blow some of the rain water through the seals of the window. A thin stream was pooling up on the floor in the light just beneath Eugene's stocking feet. The lightning flashed and filled the room with light. Eugene's big toe on the right foot twitched. The body, struggling to stay alive, kicks at death furiously. Eugene was losing more specters to the storm. His body wishes to breathe one more breath. The body rebels against dying and struggles to the last second. Eugene's right foot kicks for one last time, alone in the dark cell.

Previously published by *Downstate Story* 2013

Mentor

Eighty miles an hour on the hill roads with the top down on a 68 Ford Fairlane was not conducive to cigar lighting. All I had was my old Zippo. It was a clear night and Iris insisted on keeping a velocity consistent with the current summer temperature.

"This isn't working." I studied her silhouette in the darkness. The speedometer light reflected in her brown eyes. Shoulder length hair spun in the breeze like a shadow demon.

"Can you manage a Marlboro?" she asked.

I did while holding her notebook in front of my face. The eight track clicked to the beginning of the tape. The twilight cruise was like a roller coaster ride.

The notebook came to mind. "Don't you ever write anything happy?"

"You talkin' about my poetry book?"

"It's all about death, every poem." Iris gave me a sidelong glance.

"What would be happy?"

"I dunno. Does it always have to be so dark?

"There are only two things to write about, death and sex."

I chuckled. "Are you thirsty?"

"There's beer in the trunk."

"Warm?"

"Of course."

Iris stopped the car on the side of the road and handed me the trunk key.

"I'll take one too," she said.

I found a case of Red Stripes in the trunk and managed two bottles from the box.

"Wait a minute," I said after slamming the trunk down. "There is more to life than death and sex."

"You didn't ask about life. But there are only two things to write about, death and sex."

"That's bullshit."

Iris put out her cigarette and popped the top off the beer. I got the side long glance again as she took a long drink from the bottle. She turned in my direction.

"I don't buy it," I said.

"All poetry, music lyrics, or fiction is either about sex, or it's about death."

"What about that last song?"

"Elton John?" she asked.

"The tiny dancer song. I like that one."

"She's dead."

"Who?

"The tiny dancer."

"No."

"I'm just trying to enlighten you." She slowly emphasized each syllable when she said enlighten.

"It's just about some girl."

"Don't you listen to the lyrics?"

"You're dark."

"I just come right out and say it. Why sugar-coat everything?"

I got the Zippo to stay lit before Iris accelerated to law breaking speed again. She topped the hill before us at eighty miles per hour. I couldn't wait for the drop down the other side, into the stomach plummeting darkness at the bottom of the hill. And then on to the next. I closed my eyes, took a drag from my cigar.

"See there?"

"What?"

"You're doing it right now."

"What's that?" I asked. I turned my head to look at her silhouette again. I couldn't see her lips move, or her eyes sparkle, or her brow furrow into a serious line. But I heard her, in a surreal way, just a gentle voice.

"Writing about death."

Previously published by *Bluffs Literary Magazine* 2016

Midnight Spades

Meds are not passed until after the night's play. Everyone understands this, and everyone knows why. Twelve players usually show. Six teams of two which means we start with three games to five hundred points until the last two teams. By that time the side bets are in full swing. People put up everything from potato chips to hydrocodone. Seems like it's always the schizoaffective against the bipolars. The major depressives don't have the staying power and the PTSD sufferers don't have the attention span to count tricks. I am the only borderline personality disorder, I'm staff, and I have the narc key.

I pair up with a schizophrenic named Faye. A tall dark skinned beauty closer to my age than the rest of the young crowd. She knows the game, built our strategy, and consistently seems to know how much trump I have in my hand.

Faye was staring at me with her best poker face. It's Wednesday and we haven't made it to the championship game in weeks. She usually has her Haldol by two and is fast asleep by two thirty. But here we sat, inquiring eyes peeking over the top of our cards. All of my spades on the left side of the hand, per usual. And her eying me up, ascertaining the amount of trump I hold. By the twinkle in her eye she's holding pretty heavy too.

"Thirteen," Faye announces. A bold move since we bid first.

"By yourself?"

"Together."

I shake my head negatively. The bipolars we were playing would need one trick to set us. I don't care for that strategy.

"That's enough table talk," warns one of the women from

the other team. A young women, just a girl actually. Bright red dyed hair with a pierced bottom lip. "Just bid."

Sometimes it takes up to four hours to get the tournament concluded. A few times until sun up. There are always a couple who wig out by that time from lack of PRNs. But that was the rule. We all abided by it. Better to play wonked out than to be under the influence. Everyone agrees to stay frosty, suck ecigs, and drink all of the Mtn Dew required to finish up the tournament. Sleep is for the daytime.

If the state lackeys ever walked in at two in the morning they would be very surprised. But what could they say about a group of card playing mental misfits not sleeping? There really is nothing wrong that we are doing. We aren't up dropping ecstasy and hitting each other with hammers. It's a card game, nothing more. It's spades, and it's everything.

"Five," I say. I hold seven.

"Eight," Faye adds. So she means to go through with this strategy of hers.

Faye takes the first trick with the ace of clubs. I take the next one with the king. A smirk curls up at the ends of her mouth. I begin to stop doubting.

Previously published by *Bluffs Literary Magazine* 2018

The Go Girl

"I'm not what you would call socially proficient."

"I know the feeling," Kori said. "I hate these group projects."

"It's always the same," Zach pointed out. "One person takes charge. Someone does all the work. And there's the ones who do little to nothing."

"That's us," Kori laughed.

"But we're here. I'm giving them another fifteen minutes."

"Then we go to my car and get high."

The coffee house that was chosen for the meeting was small and overcrowded. The music filling the room was corporate and ghastly.

"What is this shit they're playing?" Kori complained.

"It's called coffee-shop. It's an actual genre."

She grimaced. Kori was twenty years Zach's junior. They spent the past semester in abnormal psych class together. She always dressed the same. T-shirt, Vans, skinny jeans, and a brown slouch beanie. Zach always looked old and haggard, somehow adorable. The worse he looked the more she was enamored of him.

"That's the key phrase. For me it will be, 'Kori, I need to go now'. That phrase activates the plan. Not a text message, or phone call. It has to be face to face. We have to be able to look the other in the eye and say it."

"Sign on the line and I own you for two years."

Natalie handed a pen to Kori. She looked at Zach with apprehension on her face. Her small pouty mouth drawn up, grey eyes intense, blonde hair protruding from under her hat. Natalie also slid the three million dollar check across the desk in her direction.

"I'm in," Kori declared. She extended her pinkie finger

in his direction. Zach attached his same finger to hers. She let go, signed the contract, swooped up the check, and made a hasty exit alone.

"That was interesting," Natalie observed.

"She's in."

"You guys have some deal?"

"To make the money…"

Natalie gave him a discerning look. Something didn't sit right with this. But she had no choice. The project was on, and Kori seemed to be "in".

"So what's the deal with this place?" Kori asked.

"I bought this," Zach answered. "With the payoff for my novel."

"Kinda bleak…"

"Well I haven't moved in yet. But it's everything I ever wanted. Two story farm house surrounded by cornfields, ten miles away from the nearest neighbor. Wrap around porch. Woods with a stream on the property. Diesel powered generator, wind and solar energy. No phone or Wi-Fi."

"You got some poor girl held hostage in the basement?"

"It's a safe house Kori."

"Now I am creeped out."

"Listen, before we catch the plane we have to talk. All the popular mean kids from high school graduated and moved to LA. That's where we're going. That's who we're working with. You can act as tough as you want but it's not our kinda place."

"We'll have a contract right?"

"It won't be enough. We need a plan. We need to make a promise to each other."

Kori burst into the apartment, interrupting the impromptu meeting Natalie had called. She was crying, sobbing, black mascara running down her face. Red lipstick was smeared on her mouth, cheeks, and chin. Small drops of blood splattered her white strapless evening gown. She stopped in front of Zach and composed herself momentarily. "I'm going to get cleaned up."

"Could you grab my sunglasses on your way out?"

Kristen looked astonished at Zach. "Sunglasses?"

"I need them."

"Are you heartless? Go see what's wrong with her.

Where the hell was she?"

"Some photoshoot or video thing. Looks like it went foul."

"She needs you."

"She'll come get me when she needs me."

"You guys are so weird. I need to go find out what happened."

"Leave her be."

"She's clearly messed up."

"She's the strong silent type. She knows what to do."

"Sunglasses…"

Zach looked at Kristen and hoped his angst wasn't showing. Kristen was the strong silent type too.

"She's gay you know."

"That doesn't make this right. Gays need people to check on them too. You fuckers share this apartment. Sleep in the same bed. I thought you were pretty tight."

"It's a big bed."

Everyone was silent for a few very long moments. They could hear the shower running through the walls.

"It doesn't matter how gay she is." Natalie finally broke the silence. "In the middle of the night when you're scared and it's dark, you reach out for the person next to you. I know how this works. Her arms around your chest. Those perky twenty year old boobs pressed up against your hairy back. Hot anxious breath on your neck."

“Hang out at the barbershop long enough and you’re bound to get a haircut,” Kristen quipped.

Zach lowered his eyes trying to not give anything away. He knew Kori was finished and what was coming. He did like these people. He wanted the meeting to continue, wanted them to keep the creative juices flowing. Working out the details of the project. The love of his life, his first novel, eventually could come to life on the big screen.

“You hate it here don’t you?” Natalie asked. “You Midwesterners are all the same. Just can’t take the heat.”

“I made it a year. I can go another.”

“What about Kori?”

“You’re that writer guy.” Kori said matter-of-factly.

“I am?”

“The one my English teacher is always talking about. You just sold the rights to your novel to some big studio in Hollywood?”

“It sounds sinful the way you say it.”

“Aren’t you excited?”

“It was actually optioned by a small production company that contracts for a big studio. I’m not excited, cause I have to fly out there. A condition for the sale is that I sign on as a creative consultant.”

“Wow! You need an assistant?”

“What I need is an executive proxy,” Zach declared.

“Like an assistant?”

“No. There’s plenty of those out there on the west coast. I need someone to work on the project and be able to make executive decisions and take creative action on behalf of the project. Someone smart and badass like yourself, who I can trust.”

“So we’ll have to work pretty closely together?”

“No again. We’ll work for Natalie who heads the production company. We really won’t need to talk or see each other.”

"I don't understand."

"I have… anxiety issues. I may not always be able to attend meetings, especially with the suits from the studio. Natalie won't hire me without a backup. An executive proxy. Someone who can fill in at any time to do my job."

"Wow."

"Yeah, and I think you'll do perfectly. I get to choose, but Natalie will have the final word."

"But I don't need to work with you?"

"We can talk, we can be friends. But she really wants someone able to act on their own who understands the project."

"No packing or saying goodbye. We stand up and leave no matter what's happening. We go together to the storage unit and get the go bag, pay cash for a used nondescript car, drive away."

Kori entered the room. Black t-shirt, Vans, and skinny jeans. Her familiar brown slouch beanie on her head. Sunglasses covered what her eyes gave away. "Zachery, I need to go now."

"I should have seen this coming," Natalie declared.

Kristen's jaw dropped. "She's your go girl."

"This is a mistake, Zach." Natalie threatened. "You walk out that door and your contract will be nullified. The project will proceed without you!"

Zach stood and put on his sunglasses, he had a promise to keep. They opened the door to the bright California afternoon and left the meeting, never to be seen again.

Previously published by *MidAmerican Fiction & Photography* 2015

Transgressive Therapist

Little Gehenna wearing dark framed glasses
opens the window to her office
feels the cold breeze through short black hair
and the sunshine on her face

a white tank top shows off dark tattoos
two full sleeves of ink
left arm seven crows
right arm ten magpies

this is her time for him
she crosses out the hour
squeezes the diary against her chest
a tear is held within tiny dark eyes

Little Gehenna sneaks a smoke
just as they once did
with her office door closed
who the hell will care?

One drag for sorrow
two for joy
three for girls
four for boys
five for silver
six for gold
seven for his secret never to be told

Casey held tenaciously to the steering wheel as his small Chevy S10 fell on a ninety-degree angle toward the ice-covered river below. He could see the bridge above disappear as he plummeted backwards to the river. The wind was blowing the snow sideways at least forty miles per hour, causing extremely poor visibility and the predicament he currently found himself in.

In the few seconds during the drop, Casey had the presence of mind to start rolling down the driver's side window after unbuckling the seat belt and hugging the wheel. The truck was going to hit hard. He hoped the impact didn't knock him unconscious. He was thinking about taking off his winter coat when the car hit the two-inch thick ice covering the river.

The impact jolted him. He managed to keep hold of the steering wheel but the collision was a shock to his system. Everything went black for a moment as he passed out from the crash. He came to, and all was a silent blur, like the stillness in the air between the heaves of a storm. He heard the stumbling buzz of a fly, and was confused. When he could see again he noticed water pouring through the window and the truck about to go under. Without thinking, he ripped his coat off and held it before him as he pushed through the window. The ice-cold river enveloped him and tugged at his body, trying to pull him under with the truck. With one arm he swung the coat above his head and onto the ice above. It stuck immediately and held him in place.

Casey could see his S10 dropping into the cold darkness below him. The coat was flash frozen to the ice above his head. He wondered where all of his strength was coming from as he pulled himself out of the water and onto the ice. In the seconds following, he began to experience the flash freeze, which had stuck his coat to the ice. He was in the middle of the river; he had little probability of having easy access to the shore. To his left was the city. To his right the shore was natural and would give access to the freeway and possibly traffic. He made a quick decision and ran toward the shore on the right.

Months later Gehenna sat still in her office and studied Sarah, a petite blond woman no bigger than herself. Unhappy; she thought she read that expression, just for a moment. Sarah sat still and quiet, like it might be a competition between the two of them. It made Gehenna feel uncomfortable.

"So what's with the bird tattoos," Sarah observed. "Those are tattoos right?"

"They're from an old poem," Gehenna replied. She wasn't about to cast her pearls.

"Did Casey know about the poem?"

This was a hint of what Casey sometimes alluded to in past sessions, competition and childishness. Did Casey know indeed? Casey knew enough for their relationship to almost be an affair of sorts. Unprofessional on her part, she knew. She gave too much to him.

"About the tattoos? Did you tell him?"

Gehenna did not reply. Instead she wrote on the intake form.

"I hate this bitch…"

Casey was beginning to freeze. His legs and arms were stiff under the coat of ice covering his clothing. The bridge was to his right so he had no problem keeping his direction in the blowing snow, but the shoreline seemed too far away. If the ice even held while he ran he was still afraid he would freeze before reaching any warmth. He thought he remembered blacking out at one point, like a flash of shadowy light in his eyes. Dizziness and nausea washed over him and he was sure it was over for him. Then he stepped onto the shore!

The shoreline would lead to the freeway on his right. It was hard for Casey to keep his breath, but he knew to stop was to die. He couldn't believe he was still alive at this point. The temperature was just above freezing; he remembered from the radio before the accident. But the wind was so strong it had to be fatal in this cold.

Casey's eyes were tearing. The wind was blowing strong in his face. His limbs were burning, aching from the exertion. It took all his concentration to keep moving. It was like trying to run through wet cement. The wet trousers and flannel shirt were weighing him down, feeling like an extra hundred pounds as he plodded along, but he decided it was safer to keep moving than to stop to take his wet clothes off. They were most likely frozen by now anyways. It would be a troublesome task, which could possibly kill him.

The smell of exhaust fumes touched his nostrils before he heard the low grumbling of many engines running at once. Suddenly it dawned on him what was happening. He could envision the overturned jack-knifed truck on the bridge. Confusion and backed up traffic to this point, probably farther, and in this weather. The snow was blowing so it was hard to see a few steps in front of him. But he realized when he started up the incline he was at the freeway. He was there, somehow, and he was going to survive, maybe.

The incline was tough to manage. It was just steep enough to make him slip if he didn't watch his footing. It was slow going and his body began to cool off in the wind. He was scared. He may not make the highway at this rate, so close to possible survival, yet falling short at the finish line. His eyes were closed, they might as well be, he couldn't see anyways. His eyelids felt as though they were freezing.

All at once the terrain evened out. Casey heard the loud

honking of a car horn to his direct left. He rubbed at his face with the palms of his hands, forcing the lids to break free and move of their own accord. He turned left. An old dark blue van was within arm's reach. He was directly in front and could see a woman at the wheel. Suddenly Casey was confused. Who was this? Where was he? The horn honked again. He watched the woman in the van waving to him, beckoning him to the passenger door of the van.

She was not alone on the highway. Cars were in front and behind, lined up from the accident on the bridge to as far back as he could see. Windshield wipers were slapping back and forth, headlights dimming as they became covered with snow. He heard the sound of a car honking, then the creak of a door opening. "Get in here!" a female voice shouted. He followed the voice, to warmth. Casey could feel heat. His body relaxed, eyes closed. He was going out fast and he knew it.

"What are you doing out there man?" the female voice asked.

"There are a lot more of those people lately," Sarah observed.

"People?" Gehenna asked.

"You know what I mean. Mental."

"That's not a real nice thing to say," Gehenna corrected.

"It's what they say in other countries."

"It's disrespectful,"

"Well there are more, seems like more than usual,"

"Maybe it's always been like this," Gehenna observed. "Maybe mental illness has always affected the same percentage of people all through time. We have the internet now, the media, and hundreds of movies about mentally ill people."

"What would you think if that wasn't true?" Sarah countered. "Half of my friends are on anti-depressants.

Most I've known since grade school. They never seemed crazy before. Something happened when they grew older."

"They weren't crazy?" Gehenna asked. "I remember young people acting insane, girls getting murdered in cars, guys shooting each other over a bag of weed, kids overdosing in school. I still say the percentages are the same."

"Well what I really want to know about is Casey, the Hero." Sarah rolled her eyes without realizing it. Gehenna felt a little nauseated at her contemptuousness. "Do you think, just between you and me, that maybe he went over the edge on purpose?

"I mean, he was distant, depressed, for the longest time. I felt like I had to nag him to do anything, especially to go to work in the morning."

"We were in negotiations, the two of us. I also thought Casey suffered from depression. I thought he needed to see a psychiatrist and get on some meds. Something to help him get a better perspective."

"Perspective on what?' Sarah asked.

"His life," Gehenna answered. "He wasn't very happy with his life."

"Was he suicidal?"

"I don't believe he was."

"I just don't get it then," Sarah said, showing a rare sliver of vulnerability. "I was part of his life. If there was something wrong with his life then there was something wrong with us."

"Not wrong," Gehenna explained. "Wrong is not a good word to use. I don't think Casey found anything wrong with his life. He was just chronically unhappy. Like an illness. Like he had a virus that wouldn't go away."

"I understand that depression is a disease," Sarah commented. "I just never related it to Casey."

"He wasn't so sick that he couldn't get out of bed. I have

many patients who are that way. He was not that far gone, yet."

"So what about us?" Sarah asked, showing all of her cards finally. "How did you see our relationship, based on what he said?"

"I don't judge such things," Gehenna lied. "And now it's time for us to change the subject."

Casey passed out. When he awoke he was still in the van, the girl looking over him.

"Hello?" she asked. "Are you awake?"

Casey stared at her blankly. He could not hear her talking. Instead, he heard the annoying incessant buzzing of a fly. The woman was dark haired. Her shadowy deep brown eyes added to the fierceness of her look. His first instinct was not to trust her. Then she smiled. The buzzing ceased, he heard the woman's voice.

"My name's Alex," she announced. "And you're Casey. I know this 'cause I've already been through your stuff." Casey smiled. He felt intoxicated and figured it was from the instant comfort of Alex's warm van.

"I shook you awake 'cause you need to get out of these clothes now. They're stiff and frozen. You're gonna get frost bite or hypothermia, or something." Alex was tugging at his pants. Casey could barely feel what was happening. She may be right about the frostbite.

"Wiggle your ass out of those pants," Alex instructed. Casey closed his eyes and tried to pull his pants over his rump. Modesty was the last thing on his mind. He knew Alex was right and he was in a bad way. After both of them struggled enough, the pants managed to come off and the shirt was removed.

"Hold on," Alex said. "I have a blanket in the back."

"Where are we?" Casey asked.

“Still at the foot of the bridge,” Alex explained. “Nothing has moved for about half an hour. Why do I think this has something to do with you?”

“Is it still snowing?” Casey asked.

“Snowing and blowing.” Her face appeared above his head, slightly smiling. Casey felt the warm blanket cover him. She started rubbing his legs and arms. He felt okay. He felt like he might survive. Where Alex rubbed his legs felt hot, like his nerve ends were thawing. It was slightly painful, but it wasn’t long before he was sitting up in the passenger seat. Alex was in the driver’s seat opening a thermos. Hot steam rolled out of the top when she was finally successful. She poured some into the screw on cup.

“It’s black coffee,” she said as she handed the cup to him. Casey gratefully accepted it and took a long drink.

Alex stared at him like she was trying to decide something. She held a finger up for him to wait a second and silently moved to the back of the van where she hunted through her bags. It looked to Casey like she was traveling somewhere, packed up and on the move. But there were only a couple bags and a few cardboard boxes in the back, which might even have been empty.

“Here,” she said after returning to the driver’s seat. Alex removed the screw top on a dark bottle, which looked like it held some kind of medicine. She took his coffee cup and slowly poured some liquid into his cup, holding it carefully in front of her face so she could judge the amount coming out of the bottle.

“Elixir of terpenhydrate,” she explained as she watched the thin stream of liquid going into the coffee. “It’ll make you feel better and sweeten your coffee at the same time.” She smiled as she handed back the cup. Casey took a sip, and then swallowed down the rest.

"So," Alex started, "what's the deal with you, Casey?"

"Fell off the bridge," Casey explained.

"Hold on. Traffic's moving." Alex had to start the van, put it into gear, and step on the gas to move a few feet on the snow covered expressway.

"Six feet!" she exclaimed. "That's all we move after thirty minutes?"

"There was an accident," Casey explained. "A semi jack-knifed, the trailer fishtailed and almost pushed a car with a mother and her two young girls inside over the edge of the bridge and into the river."

"Good God," Alex said. "What happened?"

"I rammed them with my truck and took the hit instead. They were pushed out of the way."

"You're a hero!"

"I don't think so, just stupid."

"Why would you say that?"

"Look what happened," Casey explained.

"You saved a family, survived the icy river, and now you're naked here in my van."

Casey wrapped the blanket a little tighter. The traffic moved, surprising Alex. She popped the van into gear and started pulling ahead onto the bridge.

"I can see flashing lights up ahead," Alex said.

"That must be the accident scene."

"They must think you're dead by now."

"I don't doubt it. Sarah will sure be mad."

"Sarah your wife?"

"Estranged," Casey explained. "But not so much that she won't be angry about me dying."

Sarah looked thoughtfully out Gehenna's open window, her long golden hair falling back behind her shoulders. Green eyes gave no clue to the determination lying behind them.

Casey's therapist studied the woman's poker face. She hid herself with a perfection sharpened by years of cultivation. A lifetime of dark purpose tucked away into the recesses of her personality. Casey really had no clue as to the depths of this woman's heart. Gehenna knew this now, and was repulsed. The woman had the stench about her of someone who always got what she wanted.

Sarah looked down at her feet. Something caught her sight out of the corner of her eye, a dirty ashtray and a pack of filtered cigars lying on the floor partly under an end table. "Red Bucks?" she asked. "Are these yours?"

"I guess I forgot to clean up after myself," Gehenna explained.

"Casey smoked Red Bucks. I hated that. It made him stink and cough."

"It's a nasty habit."

"I was always under the impression that those were hard to find."

"Oh no," Gehenna lied. She tried to cover the guilt in her voice. She swallowed. "They're everywhere."

"Humph," Sarah replied. "Kind of an outdoorsy type of smoke for a young woman like yourself."

"They're…" Gehenna's voice cracked just the tiniest bit. "They're vanilla flavored."

They inched up toward the top of the bridge. Alex seemed thoughtful.

"So how is life treating you, Casey?" she asked.

"Not good today," he answered.

"How about before today? In general?"

"It's a shit sandwich."

"'Cause you are at the bottom of the river for all they know. If we drove past and didn't stop, well you would just be missing and presumed dead. The river will thaw in a couple months, they will find your truck, and assume you're on your way to your final resting place somewhere south in the heart of the Mississippi."

"Why would I do that?" Casey asked.

"A new start? A chance at a better anonymous life?"

"So where would you drop me to start this new life? With no money, ID, or clothes for that matter."

"Well here's the thing, Casey. I stole this van. If I stop there's a chance the police will run the plates and figure out I'm not the owner and I'm two states away from where I'm supposed to be."

"You some kind of criminal?" Casey asked.

"Some kind," she answered.

They didn't speak again until cresting the top of the bridge. The confusion of the accident scene was cooled by the time they arrived and people were gathering around each other while others worked intently to keep the traffic moving. The woman and her two children stood alongside their vehicle. She held the hand of the smaller child, who was holding the hand of her older sister. The woman looked as though she had been crying the entire time. She had a blanket from some caring EMT wrapped around her, and she dotted her eyes with the corner of it. The children looked about with lost expressions, holding tight to each other.

"Keep driving," Casey ordered. Alex slowly accelerated along with the rest of the rubberneckers.

"Look at me," Alex said. Casey was staring out of the window, half paying attention to the effort to clear the bridge, half watching the ice on the river below. He had just been here a few hours before, or was it a lifetime. Whatever she had put into his coffee was working on him. He felt warm and euphoric. He pulled the blanket closer around his naked body, enjoying the softness against his skin.

"Casey," Alex snapped. He turned his head around and

met her gaze. She stepped on the brake. “Dead is dead. If I keep moving you move beyond this life. Look me in the eyes and tell me what to do.”

Alex had the most penetrating dark eyes Casey had ever seen, yet they were friendly and inviting. Her hair was short and dark, black framing a round face, her eyes intense as she stared at him. She struck him in that moment as a kind of dark angel, or a friendly daemon. She had put a spell on him with a most congenial potion. He smiled inside and looked through her eyes searching her purpose. Did he see something genuine? Something he had not seen in quite some time?

“Dead is dead,” Casey whispered.

“I won’t dump you,” she promised. “I’m with you as long as you need me.”

“Please keep driving,” Casey asked without removing his gaze. His eyes welled up as he stared into her dark depths. A single tear fell down his check. “Please keep driving.”

Alex slowly accelerated, and rewarded Casey with a large heartwarming smile. She had dimples set deep into her rounded cheeks. Her eyes changed to sparkling brown as she turned forward to see the road ahead. She nodded her head positively. “I won’t dump you,” she reiterated, still holding onto the smile.

“You wouldn’t happen to have any smokes, would you?” Casey pleaded.

Alex dug around in the left pocket of her coat and produced a pack of filtered cigars. “Red Bucks,” she announced. “Vanilla flavored.”

“Let’s just put this delusion of yours to rest.”

“What does that mean?” she had a fading smile. “Gehenna? Did I pronounce it right?” Gehenna had to admit to herself that Sarah had a pretty face. She could see Casey being suckered in by this one, this controlling person, lacking charisma, who probably had never been in love.

"It means Casey is dead. Case closed. Yes, a hero. I've archived his file and stored it in my drawer. It means I don't have to talk about Casey again. I don't have to think about him ever again. I can concentrate on my other clients.

"You were married to him. He was your husband and he was a good man. Unhappy, but good. Whatever occurred in the marriage was between you two. I know little of your relationship. It's yours to honor or disdain. I truly believe that if there was a way to survive the fall off the bridge, Casey would have found it. He was not suicidal.

"Now, are you paying cash on your way out? We're into this for twenty minutes. Are you leaving or do you plan on staying and paying for the rest of the hour?"

Previously published by *Penny Shorts* 2015

Asha

The ambulance came to a stop at the small Midwestern town ED doors. A doctor waited for Zach to be removed from the vehicle. So did others. People in suits, men and women, representatives and technicians for American Therapeutic Corp. Zach could smell the humidity in the cold spring morning air. It was early, the sun hadn't risen yet.

"This shit always happens at night," Zach thought to himself. The few times he had ever had to make use of the city ED had never been during daylight hours.

The young Asha was a faint voice in the dark morning. She kept herself quiet and spoke in hushed tones. "Don't take the drugs."

"I'm in pain," Zach argued. "I can't hide it. There really is no choice for me."

"I might be lost…"

"They are here Asha, the techies." Zach saw the concern on the people's faces, the ones wearing the suits with laptops tucked under their arms.

The IV had already been started by the EMTs on the way to the city hospital. Nurses waited with syringes and plungers to shoot the pain numbing drugs into Zach's system. There were lots of raised voices, hurried speech. This had never occurred before. Everyone was curious as well as concerned.

"There is an ethical dilemma here to consider," a woman said. She was smartly dressed in a modern suit, brown skin, dark eyes, a dark dot over her third eye. "We have lost Asha, his therapist."

"He is my main concern now," said a young man, the ED doctor who had taken charge of the situation. Dark rim glasses and short cropped hair. *Clark Kent*, Zach thought to himself. Asha giggled. She understood the reference.

"The pain must be addressed."

“The pain is our only link to the therapist.” Laptops had been opened and Zach could hear the tapping of fingers on cheap plastic keyboards. He saw the needless spot light from above. They had him in a trauma room. He felt his own twinge of fear. Much was happening all at once.

The twenty nine year old Zach had been relaxing in the tub when the pain attacked him. The pain was what they could measure. The pain registered then, anxiety and fear did now. The uncontrolled crying made no sense to the scientific professionals, so they ignored it. Assumed it stemmed from the pain. He made no mention of it. The woman in the suit suddenly appeared in his line of sight. She looked at him sternly. She knew.

“Only a weak dose of Benzos.”

“I can’t ignore the extremity of the pain. He could go into cardiac arrest. It must be controlled.”

“Wait until we’ve reversed the connection.”

“How long?”

Zach was aware of a nurse at his head fiddling with the IV. He careened his neck up for a view but the nurse was out of his line of vision. He looked back down to Clark Kent who quickly nodded his head in approval. Seconds later Zach felt the relaxation wash through his system as the Benzo was shot through the IV.

“Please no,” Asha pleaded.

“Don’t you want some relief?”

“I don’t want to die. If I get lost I will die.”

“Connection established,” came the voice of a male techie. More tapping on keyboards. The room was filled with anxious concentration. “Ready for reversal.” The tone had a hint of shock, like he wasn’t expecting things to be so easy.

“It’s all wireless?” asked the doctor. The dark skinned woman nodded positively. She still had her eyes on Zach.

“She’s scared,” Zach informed her.

"We know…"

In a sudden instant, after more than two years of contact, Asha was gone. Zach felt a sudden loss, emptiness. The woman put her hand on his shoulder. "I'm a therapist. I'll walk you through this."

Clark Kent nodded again and Zach was awash with the euphoric relief of opioids coursing through his blood.

"Asha?"

"Zach?"

"Rest…"

"I wanna see this thing," the doctor contemplated aloud. "Let's get him to x-ray…"

"No x-ray," came a rising of voices from the techs. "I wouldn't x-ray. Don't radiate the chip. No. No radiation. Can't x-ray."

"What do I do then?"

"Let us handle it. We have the chip under control. We are pinpointing her location now."

"It's about the size of a peanut," the dark skinned woman said. She tapped Zach on the forehead. He smiled wistfully. "Right under the frontal bone."

"Is he in danger?" Mr. Kent asked.

"The ethical dilemma," the woman reminded him. "He took on a portion of danger by agreeing to this connection. She has kept him alive these past two years, now it's his turn to save her."

"I'm scared," came Asha's voice in Zach's head.

"I know. I am too. I think everyone is. But they are all working very hard."

"I can't tell how you feel…"

"The chip has been reversed. You're scared. It's dark."

"There's no light."

"And it smells. I hear a baby crying in the distance."

"I'm too young to die."

"Asha, you won't die. The consensus is that you were abducted by human traffickers. Pretty common in the neighborhood where you live."

"I want to be near my family."

"You don't have to explain for me."

"It's like we are the only people in the world."

"That's not true. The room here is packed. You are being located. Helicopters will be deployed!"

"So what's your story?" The ED doc asked.

"Personality disorder," the ATC woman answered.

"And depression," Zach added. "Deep dark depression with anxiety; suicidal ideation."

"And you can afford the ATC chip?"

"Beta testing. I'm a test subject. Small percentage of survival. Can that damn light be turned off?"

"This is a last resort situation," the ATC woman explained. "Everything had been tried including electroshock therapy. Meds don't work on personality disorder. But Zach has responded well to the intense therapy provided by the chip."

"How's the pain?" Dr. Kent asked.

"Gone now that the chip is reversed. She wasn't just kidnapped…"

"We know," the dark woman said.

"I hear things," Asha whispered. "Gunfire. Helicopters?"

"The Indian police. Stay put. They know exactly where you are."

"That's reassuring." She was sobbing quietly.

"You're much younger than I thought."

"Good job," the ATC woman said. "Keep talking. She has known you for two years now. Your voice is reassuring."

"Tell her to get away from the door," ordered an anonymous tech.

"Asha, get away from the door."

"The gunfire is getting closer."

"Go to the farthest corner of the room, away from the door."

"I'm scared…"

"Make yourself small. Curl up into a little ball with your back to the door. Cover your head." Zach's eyes were closed tight while he gave these instructions. The doctor and the brown skinned woman looked at each other, concerned.

There was an explosion. Asha remained curled into a tight ball. Strong hands grabbed her, picked her up; ran. Zach heard the sound of helicopter blades slapping at the air. She rose straight up.

"I don't fly Asha!" Zach's eyes were still shut tight. His breathing came in gasps.

"Thanks Zach," came the still small voice in his head.

"Totally selfish on my part Asha. You know good therapists are hard to find."

Previously published in *SciPhi Journal* October 2016

Smol Boi

Ellie sat at her desk watching a live stream of Kira attempting to sleep displayed on her laptop screen. She was restless and fitfully twisting in her sheets. A message alert popped up hiding Kira's bare restless leg.

"Is your sewing machine set up?" It was Abby, who was supposed to be at Ellie's house a half hour ago. Ellie was resentful that Abby was seventeen and able to drive, yet still insisted on walking the half mile to Ellie's house.

"Yeah," she typed.

"Can I use it?"

"Of course stoopid!"

The window closed and Ellie continued watching Kira, trying to will her to restful sleep through the internet wires. By the time Abby arrived Kira was out, though once in a while her body would flinch like she was having a bad dream.

"What are you getting into today?" Abby asked.

"I wanna redo my Kanaya," Ellie answered.

"Don't fucking do anymore Homestuck." Abby's dark eyebrows furled together as she frowned. This leant a cartoonish look to her round face that was made to mostly display smiles with deep dimples that extended out to smile crevices, like parentheses for her mouth.

"Everyone's doing Homestuck again, and I got all the shit. It's a lot and it was expensive. I still like her and I ain't throwin' all this away."

"You're not even a Virgo."

"I am in my heart."

"Pisces."

"I don't give a shit. I made a damn papier mâché chainsaw. Shit! Why did I even marry you?"

"Have it your way," Abby resigned. "I'm finishing up

my OC. He's a smol bean boy with no parents and the ability to detect vampires. I need your sewing machine to finish fringing the cape."

"Everyone can detect vampires as soon as they bite into your wrist."

"See! That's the attitude from the Homestuck community talking. You're already in character."

"Let's just chill. I'll help with your OC and wait to get into Kanaya till later."

"Sorry. That's not cool. Were you gonna shoot some content? A little song and dance?"

Ellie shook her head, "I just wanted to get into something and avoid the rest of the day."

Abby was silently thoughtful for a few minutes as she opened Ellie's sewing machine cover and inspected the set up. "Time for total truth?" She asked.

Ellie nodded in the affirmative.

"I always have my Rose in the backpack."

Ellie smiled. The bedroom was bright with sunlight from the open windows making clear the white and pink walls her parents had let her paint alone. Posters of her favorite manga characters decorated one wall along with her own creations. Mostly colorful representations of characters she'd cosplayed in the past and a few dark charcoal self-portraits.

Abby and Ellie were free of school today yet both of their parents had to work. Ellie had the whole house to herself since she was an only child. Abby was escaping three older brothers and one toddler sister, leaving babysitting to the guys for a change. Ellie never wondered why Abby had a self-harming habit. She couldn't imagine having one sibling, much less sharing living space with so many. Though she did admire Abby's brothers with distant envy.

"Let's blow off this day together," Abby offered.

"You got your wig?"

"Yeah. Always. Squiddle shirt and hip hugger skirt. Thot red lipstick."

"Always prepared like a good Homestuck scout. I didn't ever know that."

"Wanna secret?"

Ellie nodded again.

"It's a deal I made with my mom and therapist. I said I'd give up hurting myself but get to keep Rose with me, always handy."

"Your mom's pretty cool."

"She's never surprised when Rose sits next to her on the couch to watch Netflix."

Ellie felt they both were luckier than most of their friends at school. "My dad laughs at me about being such a gay boi. He's totally inappropriate, but he never gave me any shit about it. Never hated me or punished me or said anything about goin' to the camps. I promised I'd always be his little girl forever."

"That's one thing I can't do. You're lucky to be out."

"I thought you're a girl?"

"I'm gay as fuck hoe, otherwise I'd put the moves on you but you're a smol boi."

"I have all the girlie parts."

"Is that an invitation?"

"Just information. Get into Rose and maybe you'll find out who I can be a girl for."

"My manly boi," Abby quipped. "I'm so proud."

"You want to continue as my wife you'll cut this shit out." Ellie's eye brows tried to furrow but not successfully, since her brows matched her light blonde, short cropped hair. Instead her forehead formed comical wrinkles that matched the continuous bright disposition showing on her face. Ellie couldn't frown if she wanted to, but always thought she was somehow managing it and getting her point across.

"Sorry baby. I didn't mean to disrespect my platonic hubby." Abby puckered her lips and aimed a squeaky kissing sound in Ellie's direction.

Ellie started taking her street clothes off to get into her long red Kanaya skirt. "I'm going with a black fitted workout top instead of my old t shirt."

"It doesn't have the Virgo emblem," Abby observed from her seat at Ellie's desk.

"No, and I'm not wrapping my tits today either, I don't care right now. I don't know what I'll do later. I got new horns in the mail though, I haven't opened the package yet."

"Exciting!" Abby exclaimed. "What was wrong with the other ones?"

"I busted them, both, at the same time in the back pocket of my jeans." Ellie looked at her porcelain white skin in the full length mirror on her wall. She studied her arms and turned to look at her back. "I can't wait to get a tattoo."

"You're not getting a Kanaya tattoo," Abby ordered.

"Maybe…"

"Well, you have two years to decide. A lot can happen in that time." She was distracted by Ellie's laptop. "What are you logged into?"

"Live.somethin. I dunno."

"This girl's asleep."

"Yup."

Abby leaned on Ellie's desk for a better view. "Shit, everyone on this channel is asleep."

"I know."

"You're watching people sleep?"

"Yeah."

"What the hell is wrong with you?"

"It's comforting," Ellie explained. "I dunno, I just like it. It helps my anxiety, especially when I can't sleep."

"Do you do this?"

"Stream myself sleeping?"

"Yes."

"Yeah. It's like having hundreds of people watching out for you. It helps me fall asleep."

"No way!"

"Yeah dear. It really helps."

"Have you ever done that to us?" Abby inquired with anxiety.

"No. I do good streaming content. I'm not a hack!"

Abby stared thoughtfully at Kira being broadcast to the laptop screen, who was finally resting peacefully in her half lit bedroom. "I'm intrigued."

"We could do it at the same time some night. See what you think."

"I'm sleeping over tonight…"

"Do it in the same room?" Ellie acted shocked.

"Yes. In costume!"

"You want old men logging in and jerking off while we sleep?" Ellie was disgusted at the thought.

"We don't have sex!"

"We sleep all over each other. Sometimes I wake up so tangled up in a leg lock I can't get away to pee."

"I just thought it would be interesting content," Abby speculated. "You get many followers?"

"Like four hundred, sometimes six."

Abby stole another quick glance at the laptop. "This girl's got over twelve hundred."

"She's been at it a long time. She gets depressed so she spends a lotta time in bed."

"Let's try it!"

"Well we have to wear pajamas then, or our onesies.

No bare skin. The thought of pedophiles makes my skin crawl."

"But we're cosplayers!"

"We can stream cosplay all you want today, but we sleep with clothes on."

"Deal!" Abby's eyes sparkled. At first the sleeping phone cam sounded stupid, but the way Ellie explained it made her interested. There was something publicly intimate about the idea. "You use the laptop for this Live.thingy or your phone?"

"It's easier with the phone," Ellie explained.

"Let's set it up then and do our makeup."

"Cool," Ellie agreed. "You need to make an account too."

Abby watched as Ellie was now considering the snow white skin on her thigh as a canvas for her future tattoo. "I want to bite your shoulder right now."

Ellie's head spun around like she was shocked, but a large smile exploded on her face and her bright blue eyes lit up like neon. "I wanna let you."

Previously published by CaféLit 2018

Anoxic Insult

I'm a small girl of 25 years. Small being one way to describe me, boyish another. I have a hard time staying above one hundred pounds and stand all of four foot and nine inches. I'm easy for a man of medium build to pick up, and even to carry. If that man is a smoker, in bad health, and has to get me through a blizzard, I'm not sure he would survive. But miracles happen every day. Why not for us too?

"Zach did a lot of dying after that adventure," the neurologist explained. "While he was being revived his brain was not getting oxygen. When oxygen levels are significantly low for four minutes or longer, brain cells begin to die and after five minutes permanent brain injury can occur. This is called an anoxic insult. The results are random. There's no sequence of what dies first and the condition could be fatal. In Zach's case it wasn't, but many of his short term memories were destroyed. Since his last couple of years were very busy, it meant he lost the memories of many newly formed relationships.

"Longstanding relationships remained intact, causing little emotional distress for Zach. The loss of a couple years' work and those who worked with him though, doesn't come without its own acute anxiety. The comfort of long established support systems keeps the event from being disabling. He doesn't remember you Iris. To him, you've never met."

"It's important he remembers, doctor. There's a large financial price tag attached to our working relationship."

The doctor eyed me silently. She tapped her fingers on the table next to my hospital bed while I held back tears. "We can wait and see. That's all we can do. I can't promise anything. There are other types of memory. There's sensory memory, muscle memory, and emotional memory. His body may remember things that certain parts of his brain does not. He may feel a certain way in your presence that he can't explain. But we can't know. We have to wait until he is emotionally stable. And we need to get you some rest. Your inability to fall asleep is becoming worrisome."

"I have to see him."

"I forbid you to. As his doctor I need to protect his emotional wellbeing. It's important to his recovery."

"He's in this hospital though?" I asked.

"What do you think? There's no medical unit of this caliber for hundreds of miles. I'm not breaking any rules telling you so, since you can logically deduce the answer."

"Is he warm?" I don't know why I asked that. It just seemed very important in that moment.

"All of the patients in this hospital are kept warm and comfortable."

"I'm not…"

"I'll check in on you again later."

"I've logically deduced you're a bitch," I said aloud to the empty room after she left. Sleep or no, they don't know how imperative it is that I see Zach. My emotional wellbeing is important too.

I didn't wait to be "checked on later". My limp was severe but I could walk. I took this logical deduction the doctor talked about to its conclusion that Zach was on the same floor as me. The nurse's station was probably alerted to keep us apart. My plan was to wander the halls on a covert recognizance mission, peeking into rooms until I saw him. Astonishingly, he was in the room next to mine.

"Hi Zach. My name is Iris. You don't remember me. I'm not supposed to be here." He was in bed and the room empty; an IV line was attached to his arm.

"You being sneaky?"

"Very. Took me forever to steal a walking pole for my IV. They told me not to talk to you."

"A rebel…"

"Do you know why you're in a hospital bed?"

"I was told about the plane crash. And a young girl. The pilot died. You must be the girl."

"I am, and that's all true. I'm still in trouble though. High anxiety and all, haven't slept for three days. They've tried everything from sleeping pills to the date rape drug. If I don't get natural sleep soon I'm going to die. The last ditch effort is going to be a chemical coma. They think they can keep me alive that way for some time."

I tried to stare him down. Take him in with my eyes. He seemed drugged. Probably benzos.

"Don't you have pajamas?" he asked. I only had the gown given to me by the hospital. Out of habit I didn't check to see if I was appropriately covered.

"We kinda have a clothing optional type of relationship. Our people haven't figured out where we are yet to bring us clothes."

"I worry," Zach started, with his eyes closed. "I worry a lot about the truth. I have no memory of ever meeting you. I don't see why you would lie though. Maybe I'm delusional."

"You're not supposed to know this, but I'm desperate, so I need to tell you. My femur artery was severed during the emergency landing and I was losing a lot of blood fast. You found vise grips in the plane's toolbox and stopped the bleeding. Packed the wound with gauze and duct taped everything so it was solid. You took two of the plane seats apart and made a sled to pull me behind you through the storm and down the mountain. You pulled me for four hours until we were clear of the blizzard. Then the sled fell apart. You used the straps from the sled to tie me to your back and carried me for two more hours. If you hadn't I would be dead. I wasn't going to last in the plane until we could be rescued. They said over the radio my only hope was to get down the mountain below the storm ASAP."

"Seems reasonable to me. We did what we had to do. Together. We must have made a great team. I don't completely understand what we were working on together other than survival, or why I'm on the west coast instead of home. I'm a writer, so it must have something to do with that?"

"I begged you not to go out. When you first opened the door to the plane, and I saw how strong the wind was, I knew you wouldn't make it. And you didn't. You died several times after the snowmobiles showed up to rescue us. I watched as they revived you, in the snow at the bottom of the mountain. They put me on a snowmobile and drove me the rest of the way down. They had to helicopter you off the mountain. You died again in the helicopter, and again at the hospital. You obviously were revived, but now you don't remember."

I wanted that to sink in, for him to ask questions. He just stared at me awestruck.

"It was so cold Zach. The snow blew horizontally. They say the wind gusts were sometimes eighty miles per hour. There was just no way for us to survive in that. I have no idea how we did. You kept going. Stopping only to throw up, often. They had our GPS coordinates the whole time. We had reception but never talked on the phone. You hoarded every breath. You didn't waste a step.

"Actually it's a blessing you can't remember. I can't get warm. They put heated blankets on me and all I do is shiver and cry. My body is incapable of feeling warmth. My mind and emotions are stuck in that storm. I haven't felt safe since we were separated. I only feel safe here, right now."

"So we must know each other pretty well."

"The day we got on that plane was our three hundred and sixty sixth day together."

"A whole year."

"A year and a day. I remember the first three words you said to me when we met."

"That's impressive. It must have been memorable."

"I love you. That's what you said. I introduced myself, and you simply said I love you."

"How forward. I'm a cad!"

"Every day following, you told me you loved me."

Zach didn't answer.

"You told me you loved me three hundred and sixty six times. And on that three hundred and sixty sixth day you decided that my existence was more important than your life."

Zach remained silent.

"I just know that I can lose my fears in your arms. I know this because I've done it before. You don't remember and I have no idea what to do about that, but I'm not going to survive this. We're not out of the storm yet. You're not finished with me. So I'm here and I'm not really asking. This just has to happen."

"You're not alone," Zach said softly after a few contemplative moments. "I may not remember, but I feel it's important to believe you. I think you won't feel warm and safe until you're sure we are both warm and safe. Keeping us separated may have been a mistake on the part of the doctors."

"Then scoot the hell over."

Zach obliged. I grabbed his hand and wrapped his arm around myself. I immediately relaxed against his skin. In the following seconds my eyes became heavy. My core felt warmth. "I love you," I barely said before falling into a deep slumber.

Previously published by CaféLit 2018

Waking Dream

Twirling and spinning slowly, her thin skirt swirls loosely around her legs. Drops down around her ankles. Moving arms and hips slowly to the beat of the music. She dances in her own world. A drug dance sparkles in her eyes, deep set in black mascara. She is not there, and then back again. In and out, like a visitor. Always dancing to the music slowly. Perfect for her waking opium dream.

Alex's dark hair is short and not quite down her neck, but her bangs cover her eyes, unless she looks up. Which doesn't happen much because she is watching her bare feet. They tell her a story of lost love and cigarettes long gone. The opium lust hours past – minutes lost. They tell her it's like hitting the snooze button over and over not wanting to wake up, then finding out there is no need to. Her hair bounces, just slightly, because she moves slowly. And there is no need to, no matter how long the alarm sounds. Tonight she gets to roll back over and not get up. Nine till five in the morning.

Alex sat, hours after the music stopped. She can't hear him through the opium lust, the drive to dream. "You missed it?" she asks him. He thinks she is so beautiful. Her hands are firm yet slender, strong and subtle as a finger pokes the tabletop, making a point. "Missed it. It went by you. You missed it!" she announces as loud as is possible. It breaks his reverie. The sounds stop and suddenly they are the only people. Only the sound of Alex's voice remains, and her penetrating eyes deep set and dark. "You may have just missed it, right back then. The moment of change, the slight shift that no one noticed. It was your answer. Your dream comes true. Back then long ago you asked for it. Cried silently in the light of the full Moon. Begged at the feet of the Gods. And when it came you missed it. No one ever does that."

He takes a shot of espresso. Swallows it quickly back behind his tongue so he won't taste it full on. The bubble remains. No sound or interruption. Alex animated with her dark hair, matching eyes, and penetrating stares. Chin set and no smile. "If the Gods granted me my dream. Well, the list of clichés goes on and on. Be careful what you wish for. I'm totally completely one hundred percent aware."

She stands up, backs away. Her hips start to sway. The music plays. The sounds and the noise return from a place far away. It takes a while for them to catch up. The effect is surreal. He sees her lips move. "I feel sorry for you" is what it looks like. "I can make my own choices," he says, but the words don't come out of his mouth. It doesn't matter; her eyes are back on her feet. They are typing a story on the hardwood floor. Her body moves to the sound of piped in corporate coffee shop music.

She moves in her dream. I think I got my point across, he decides. I can't imagine doing better than perfection. Beyond the window the countryside appears. The city streets are a memory. Nine till five in the morning. It all just washed away. That's why we build homes of thatched leaves. Where your feet stand, that's permanent.

Previously published by *Bluffs Literary Magazine* 2018

Sunburn

"Kill me!" Iris cried. "Kill me now!"

"Iris is that you?" Zach asked.

"Any second now a foul alien creature will explode from my abdomen," Iris explained. "Kill me now before it's too late!"

"Is that Saran Wrap?" Zach asked.

"Yes," Iris answered. "I've been Saran Wrapped to this telephone pole." Her legs and feet were wrapped together and her arms were straight at her sides. She was wrapped from her ankles to her stomach; her exposed skin squashed against the transparent wrap.

"Who did this?"

"My best friend in the whole world, Vicky."

A horse fly was buzzing around Iris's face. Zach flicked his hand at it until it flew away.

"The sun will be up soon," Zach pointed out. "You're gonna get a sun burn on those white legs." The wrapping process raised the hem of her dress up so some of her thigh was exposed. "A bad enough burn and you could get skin cancer. I think Vicky is trying to kill you."

"What are you doing out so early?" Iris asked.

"Going to the Grab and Save for some smokes. How long have you been like this?"

"Since about midnight. Vicky is really pissed at me, something about a boy. She can be way too competitive."

"Aren't you going crazy out here?" Zach asked.

"I got some sleep," Iris answered. "I can see the big screen TV in the Hartman's house across the street. The African Queen was on, that's when I fell asleep."

"What's on now?" Zach asked. He turned to see.

"Looks like Bugs Bunny," Iris answered.

"There's bird shit in your hair," Zach said, not taking

his eyes off the Hartman's TV. Iris's short jet-black hair had a splash of white near the top of her head.

"That's a bad sign," Iris commented.

"Nonsense," Zach replied.

"A bird shitting on your head before the sunrise is a sign to go home and crawl in to bed for the rest of the day."

"My parents are taking the boat out on the river this morning," Zach said. "You wanna come along?"

"You know I do."

"I know you really love the river. Bring sunscreen this time if you're gonna wear one of those sun dresses. And your big goofy straw hat."

"Here comes old Mrs. Stilman," Iris said, her head turned to look down the street.

"In all of her blue haired glory," Zach chided, "and walking her mean Chihuahua. Don't ya just love small town life? Want me to stick around and make sure it doesn't piss on your boots?"

"I'll be okay," Iris assured. "You're probably dying for a smoke by now."

"Be at the marina by eight?" Zach asked.

"Wouldn't miss it," Iris answered.

Iris was right Zach wanted a cigarette bad. He meandered down the sidewalk toward the convenience store. Behind him he could hear Mrs. Stilman.

"You're going to get those snow white legs sun burned," she said. "It's supposed to be a warm day today."

"Kill me Mrs. Stilman!" Iris cried. "Kill me now!"

Previously published by CaféLit 2018

Campo del Alfarero

The thin sixty year old woman held on to her floppy sun hat as she high stepped it through the tomato patch. Kira watched from the safety of the garage as her mother ran from the sudden downpour that caught her working in the garden. She disappeared into the old farm house, and the scene became awash with rain, like the bleeding of water colors on a wet canvas.

Kira waited as the deluge passed. She turned her attention back to the mission at hand, the sorting of the contents of the garage. The twenty year old took on the task of her own accord, desiring sentimentality above order. She was also curious. Pictures of her father always made her curious. One of the reasons she was still alive was curiosity about him. The less she knew the less she wanted to die, just in case. Besides, she liked the garage. It was only five years old, clean, red, and shaped like a small barn. It was a great place for storage, as well as a place to park Ingrid's truck.

A small pile of Polaroid pictures, some faded a bit, stacked on the shelf above the shoe box she had been rummaging through. The rain slowed to a sprinkle. She eyed the small pile and decided it was enough. She scooped up the paper memories and followed her mother's route into the house. She found her, wet, sitting at the dining room table sipping red wine. Two more glasses were set out on the table. Mother was always hoping to be joined. Kira sat and poured a small amount into a glass, set the pictures down so her mother could see them.

"Sperm donor," Mother noticed.

"Della Jean," Kira started, "stop calling him that." When Kira was upset she called her mother by her first and middle names. Kira was upset.

“Well that’s what he was, honey.”

“He is my father.”

Della fell silent. She looked thoughtfully at her daughter, trying to figure out the correct thing to say. Finally deciding that correct thing was nothing.

“Sorry,” Kira apologized. “Feeling a little sentimental this afternoon. I have such vague memories of him.” “So what brought all of this on, darling?” Della asked sincerely. She took a sip of her wine and fiddled with bread on a plate before her. The round table was made of fine finished oak with flowers and a fruit bowl to decorate it. She picked a pinch of the bread and dipped it in a tiny bowl of olive oil and ate it. Kira reached over in front of her mother and did the same. Then sipped some wine.

“I think about him once in a while,” Kira answered. “Especially when I’m down.”

“Well you shouldn’t let being fatherless bring you down.”

“It’s not that Mother. I just wonder sometimes, if he is sick too. The psychiatrist says what I have is biological, and yet I’ve never seen you depressed a day in your life.”

He was sick.

“There are times that I feel a bit deprived, not having a father growing up.”

“Ingrid and I weren’t enough for you?”

Kira was silent.

“How about now?” Della asked.

“Yes now too. It would be nice to have a respectable principal male role model in my life.”

“So you assume your father was respectable?”

“You tell me.”

“Well, he was lured in by my wiles…”

“So he didn’t know?”

“No dear, not until I was pregnant,”

"That's despicable."

"Say what you wish. I've been happy with the results."

Kira finished her wine in one gulp and poured some more. Della did the same. They looked at each other silently for a few long moments. Kira's soft dark brown eyes were deep set and had too much dark mascara. She had a square jaw and a chiseled look.

"Come now. The consequences haven't been so bad," Della pleaded.

"I've had my share of boys."

"That's not what I was referring to."

"Guess I'm a lot like my dad, lured by a lover's wiles."

"Or a lot like your mother, finding similarities more with your own kind."

"I'm the apple to your tree Della Jean."

"Drink your wine, dear. You need to dull that tongue a bit."

Kira cautiously stood and left the table. She didn't want to seem to be leaving in a huff, but she was finished with the conversation. She was heading out the door when Della asked her a question. "How long has it been honey?"

"You put far too much emphasis on relationships," Kira said without turning to face her mother. She continued walking, and found she had nowhere to go except back to the garage.

It had only been a few months since her last break up. She didn't know why Mother cared so much about her love life. That one was a basket case anyways. Mother didn't understand how hard it was to find a decent girl in this area. All the good ones were straight or married. Mother didn't have to date anymore. She had spent the last twelve years of blissful whatever with Ingrid. In a rural area like this, surrounded by small towns, it was hard enough to find your kind of people, much less an available girl who wasn't a complete nutcase.

She was bored with looking for, or at, pictures of her father or anyone else. But she was also sad and empty inside. Just from thinking of her father. She needed something to do, an action to help organize her feelings. There was a notepad and a pencil on the workbench. She sat on the garage stool and wrote a letter.

By the time you read this…

I will be grown up. You will be old, and we will have had the greatest of times together. I remember the laughter, the games, and how you made me feel special. Digital media will have captured our smiles and laughter, and that will be all that I wish to remember. Because life is short, and I wish to hold onto the memories that bring me joy. That was the real you. Was it not? Our arguments were few, your discipline lenient. My heart was full of you, my spirit rested in our love.

No boy ever measured up. And that's the trick isn't it? I know this now. That by showing me how a man behaves I will have a measure of what to expect. And I've been often disappointed. But my consolation is that I didn't run off with the first one who acted like he cared about me.

This is not how it happened though Father, Dad, sperm donor. Because by the time you read this I will be filled with grief and angry with men as a whole. Caused by your sudden disappearance. And my loss. I will find solace in the boys that I previously described. I'll want for them and believe every word. And luckily not have become pregnant.

By the time you read this, I will be older, and will have learned of the disease I inherited from you. Mother made a bad choice of sperm donor. But she didn't know. Who knew back then? Medical histories don't show clinical major depression. You just buck up and carry the burden. Crawl out of bed and trudge through the day, trying to be stronger than you are, trying to be in denial, because denial is the only refuge.

Kira found the kitchen empty when she came back to the house. But dinner was cooking in the oven. She knew not what, but it smelled good, like most of Mother's food. Ingrid had been out of town for the last week. They were expecting her to return tonight. But at the moment the house was theirs. She found an envelope at the role table in the office. She put her letter in it, folded the flap in without sealing it, and wrote "mail this please" on the front, making the assumption that her mother had an address to send to.

Kira set the letter on the table and left the kitchen. She traversed the staircase to her bedroom on the second floor, passed her mother's room on the way, but saw no sign of her. Della may have been on the first floor still, or in the basement finding more wine. She felt better after writing the letter, but was nervous now at the thought of her mother reading it.

Dinner was eaten in silence. Della stopped drinking wine as soon as she saw the letter from Kira. She needed her head clear. Kira was old enough now and could be told about her father. And she displayed the same symptoms, so she needed to know.

"You're not a mistake," Della began.

Kira looked up from her plate. She swallowed before speaking. "I had never even considered that I was."

"Well what I'm about to tell you may make you think so."

Kira put her fork down and silently waited for her mother to speak.

"Your father took a trip to Mexico and never returned."

"He's in Mexico?" Kira asked.

Della took a breath and sighed. She looked her daughter in the eye, cool, poker faced. "His body is in Mexico."

Kira's eyes blinked rapidly for a bit. "What does that mean?"

"It means that the last memory you have of him is the last time any of us saw him, alive."

"So he's dead?"

Della slowly nodded her head in affirmation.

"He was found dead with enough pentobarbital in his system to bring down an elephant," she explained. "He wanted to die anonymously and disappear from everyone's lives."

"He did that to me?" Kira asked.

"He died of a disease, Kira. Just as if it had been cancer. Sure he gave it lots of thought and planning. He didn't want to just die, have someone he loved find his corpse. Burden us with a funeral and all. It was the potters grave he sought. And in the end that is what he found. Only the one mistake gave him away.

"But his thinking was clouded by illness, his desire that of his daemons. He did not wish to do anything to you, or me. He just wanted to disappear."

"So how did you find all of this out? What was his mistake?"

"A tattoo across his chest with a simple statement, 'I like to be read to'. He had that tattooed across his chest in case he was ever incapacitated and hospitalized. He wanted the hospital staff to know that he preferred to be read to."

Kira smiled. Found a chuckle to punctuate her tears. "Awesome…" she whispered.

"Some coroner in Mexico decided to check with the authorities in the states. Zach had been arrested in the past, during the NAFTA protests in Seattle. He was processed in jail, his tattoos dually noted. A match was found. Unfortunately he was buried before I was notified.

"He made sure that he died with no identification on his body. If a person does that in a foreign country they most likely wind up in some unmarked grave in a cemetery set aside for the impoverished. Plus Mexico was probably a good place to find the pentobarbital he needed. It's pretty hard to get your hands on around here."

Della became silent letting this sink in a bit. Kira picked up her fork and started picking at her food.

"He was supposed to be in your life. That was the deal we made. I insisted on having you and admitted to tricking him. He said he would go along with it but wanted to be in your life. He wanted to be your father Kira. It wasn't really that he left you. It was the disease."

"It's like that you know," Kira explained. "One day you're yourself, then it seems like the next day you're a totally different person, a person with a deep pain, deep in the chest and stomach, where it hurts and lays heavy. It's actually hard to commit suicide in that state. It's hard enough to get out of bed, much less travel to Mexico. When energy returns, and just before the emotional trauma has begun to heal, that's the dangerous time. That's when a person thinks about the downward part of the roller coaster ride, and having to relive that. It's the time when plans that were made while stuck in bed, come to fruition."

"I'm telling you this now because of the time you spent in the psych ward."

"My inheritance?" Kira quipped. She stood from the table, no longer hungry, but requiring the solace of her room, or the garage again. She stood still, deciding. A red-winged black bird charooped from outside, drawing her attention to the garage. But upstairs was her soft pillow, in case she needed to shed a few tears.

Her decision was made for her when she heard the sound of Ingrid's truck returning home. There was no reason to involve her in any of this. Let Mother do that. Kira made for the stairs.

"I don't want you going to Mexico."

The engine cut out. Kira heard the door of the truck open and then close. Another charoop from the bird. She stood at the foot of the stairs, not looking at her mother.

"Don't worry Della Jean, I would make sure that it was you who found me."

Della's cool poker face broke, her jaw dropped, and a tear rolled from her eye.

Previously published by *Downstate Story* 2018

Let's Not Pretend

"I get to be the hostess this time," the sister whined. "My name shall be Euphraise, but you will be my guest, so you can call me Euphy."

"Oh you sly one," the other sister scolded. "You have managed to steal the good name again, and here I sit, not being able to think of a thing."

Euphy finished brushing her long dark hair and checked herself in the bathroom mirror. Her reflection was slightly distorted where she had brushed away the condensation from the steam. She looked younger than she felt. Her baby face looked back at her like an impish child looking through a window.

"Well then you just stay here until something comes to mind," Euphy said. "I'll go tend to my hostess duties." Euphy left her Sister in the bedroom. She went downstairs to prepare tea. She wore an old, long, cotton, summer dress that had once belonged to her Mother. It was white and loose, and flowed around her as she descended the stairs. In the kitchen, Euphy began to prepare the tea. She opened a small box of cookies while the tea was brewing, and brought out her Mother's old china.

When she left her Sister upstairs, the girl was wearing only a long thick terry cloth robe. And her hair was still drying from the shower. Euphy lit a candelabra the decorated the dining room table. It was a nice added touch to the table setting. Plus, the sun was going down soon, and they would need the light.

"My name is Natasha," Euphy's Sister announced as she entered the room. "I'm so grateful to have you invite me to tea." Natasha was still wearing her bathrobe, but she decorated it with a string of her mother's pearls, and a huge, straw, wide-brimmed, gardening hat. The last, and most noticeable part of her ensemble, was the dark pair of Ray bans covering her eyes. Her face was framed with the same color of damp dark hair as Euphy's.

"Oooohhhh!" Euphy exclaimed. "It's so good to have you here for tea. You just sit yourself down at the table. It's almost ready." She exited the dining room, but Natasha could still hear her carrying on as she readied the tea.

"You know," she said loudly, to be heard in the next room, "my electricity has been shut off. I still have gas though. I just lost my electric bill, and it never got paid."

"Perhaps you could call them," Natasha suggested.

"Perhaps I could," Euphy said, sounding a bit winded as she entered the dining room. She carried a large silver tea set. Natasha could smell the tea in the pot. It smelled of an exotic blend of herbs and teas. "I have candles though, and the gas is still on. They won't shut that off because it's so cold outside, what with it being winter and all. But those pesky health agents keep coming to the door. I talked to them before. All they kept saying was silly stuff about mental health and sanitariums. I don't answer the door anymore. I just get too afraid that it's going to be one of them."

"So you don't mind the darkness?" Natasha just had to know.

"It's kind of fun actually," Euphy said in her best mischievous, little girl voice. "I like the shadows, and the eerie way the candle light dances around the room. It's almost like living in a haunted house."

"I'm afraid that I would miss television too much," Natasha said. "I love television. I would rather have the gas shut off. I can always wrap myself up in blankets and watch television."

Euphy poured the tea thoughtfully. Natasha helped herself to a cookie. She placed it on her plate and waited for the tea to be served.

“You have such a lovely tea service,” Natasha observed.

“I hope you can see all right,” Euphy said. “The sun is starting to go down you know.”

“I love the candle light,” Natasha reassured. “Everything is just so lovely.”

“I do miss television,” Euphy admitted. “I miss my shows. The nights seem so empty, and it’s hard to read by the oil lamps.”

“And those lamps give off such a horrid smell,” Natasha empathized.

“I think we should go downtown tomorrow morning and see about getting your electricity back.”

“A sleepover?” Euphy asked excitedly.

Natasha took off her sunglasses due to the ever increasing darkness in the dining room. She took a sip of the tea. “Scrumptious,” she said.

“It will be so cozy having you here tonight,” Euphy said.

“I’ll tell you what,” Natasha said, “let’s think up a television show of our own, and act it out tonight.”

“Like a play?” Euphy asked, excited again. “Oh yes Miss Natasha! That sounds so fun. I’m so lucky that you stopped by today. And a sleepover. Why, I haven’t had a sleepover since my Mother and Father went away. Seems like no one comes to my door anymore, except those pesky health people.”

“That’s it!” Natasha exclaimed wide eyed. “That’s our show!”

“What!” Euphy started. “What! What! Oh do tell me!”

“Okay,” Natasha began, “you know how your basement is. There’s the dirt floor and all. What we’ll do is get a shovel from your garage, and then we will lure the health agents to the basement. Let them in the house and kinda make noises and stuff so they will come down the stairs. And then…”

Just then came a knock on the door.

"Health department!" a voice shouted from the other side.

"Oh pooh!" Euphy whispered with exasperation. She blew out the candelabra. "Just when we were about to play such a nice game!"

"We can still play," Natasha whispered excitedly in the darkness. "Sneak out to the garage and get the shovel. I'll meet you downstairs."

The knocking got louder at the door.

"What are we going to do?" Euphy whispered with a scared frown. Natasha put her Ray Bans back on and smiled sweetly.

"You just get that shovel downstairs," she said, "I'll handle the rest."

"Oh, Natasha." Euphy said before leaving the room, "I love you. I just adore you. Sleeping over is such fun."

Previously published by CaféLit 2018

THE HOMELESS

The following stories have not yet been published by a magazine.

Summer Neurotransmitter Disruption

"I'm not ready to go home yet!" Phil was adamant. We were riding the trails down by the creek. He was on the upward surge of a powerful DXM high and soon would be having conversations with people who weren't there.

I wasn't high, but I was out of cigarettes. Hot and tired, the sun was topping out the afternoon sky, humidity at a hundred percent. I never understood what that meant, seems like a hundred percent humidity should be rain. Dinner tonight was at a pizza buffet. I wasn't very excited by it, but I did know that Mom would have the air conditioner on this afternoon. I longed for it and didn't want to babysit Phil as he stripped his clothes off and ran through the creek, again.

"Why do you do that shit?" I asked him.

"Go home if you like," he suggested. He stood and peddled hard on his old Schwinn. Jumped a rock and narrowly missed slipping into the creek.

"I wish your chain would snap," I said.

"You can be such a little bitch." His long blond hair was sticking to the sweat on his forehead. That far away expression was starting to surface on his face. I wish he would have thrown up.

"I can also be home in the air watching TV," I snapped.

Phil stepped off the bike and sat on a log facing the running water.

"I'll be visiting you someday in an institution, where they put you once your brain becomes so damaged that you can't stop drooling and babbling."

"You can keep my bike chain as a memorial to hang on your wall," he answered cryptically.

Sweat rolled off my hair and onto my glasses. I had to take them off to wipe them on my shirt, which would leave a big smudge so I wouldn't be able to see until I got home.

Phil stood and walked away. It was a blur, like a dream, some vision from another dimension. He was a blond robot, skinny legs protruding from dark shorts, a science fiction horror story. I tried to squint but was blinded by the bright sun reflecting from the water's surface. I didn't get to see where he went. When I replaced my glasses he was nowhere in sight.

I sat on the log where he had been seated and sighed heavily. I wouldn't leave him. I knew that. My stomach would hurt later from the heat, and I'll be in no condition for the pizza buffet.

"You'll get poison ivy again," I said out loud, just in case Phil was close enough to hear. Tomorrow I will stay home and watch Gilligan's Island reruns.

Brown Bag of Paper

The sun began to set over the Royal Crown Mobile Estate Park. A large tree grew next to mobile home number 1012, in which two squirrels played. They chased each other through the branches and up and down the length of the tall tree. It would soon be dark and one of the last of summer's "dog days" would come to an end. The traffic flew by on interstate 80 right over the fence. The squirrels didn't notice. It had been there all of their lives and was merely a background noise to them. Cars, pickups, and semi-trucks hauling trailers. The occasional song wafting through the breeze for a second as a car screamed past with its windows down.

An old Yamaha motorcycle pulled up and stopped in front of 1012. The short woman on the cycle lowered the kickstand with her boot and swung herself off. She removed her helmet and let her long strands of blonde hair fall free down her back. She removed a grocery sack from the cycles side pack and walked to the front door. She stepped through the door silently, walked to the kitchen table and forcefully set down the bag of brown paper.

"There it fucking is," she announced. Her long blonde hair fell over the shoulders of her black leather jacket. She turned a chair around and sat down on it backwards. She lit a cigarette and crossed her arms across the back of the chair. She took a long drag and blew the smoke out, looking at the others seated around the table as she did so.

"It's about fucking time, Lisa," said Woody as he eyed the bag. "You're a bit late."

Lisa ignored him and kept smoking. She knew she had the upper hand. She did the leg work on this one and she had the say in how it went. Out of everyone seated at the round kitchen table, she was the one most intimate with the details.

"Good work," said Shorty. He was called Shorty because of his above average height. He was also the lead man in the job. He got his orders from the bosses. He was the one who hired Lisa. He knew she was a live wire, but she was also a professional.

Woody reached for the bag and Don grabbed him by the wrist. "We're waitin' for Sal."

"Fuck off, cocksucker," Woody barked as he shook his wrist free.

"Waiting for Sal?" Lisa asked.

"Yeah," said Don. She was looking at Woody, even though Don answered. "Guess I'm not late then, asshole."

"You talkin' to me?" Woody asked.

"Shit yeah you ugly bastard. You said I was late"

"You are fucking late."

"But no one is doin' nothin' till Sal gets here."

"We waited a long fucking time."

Lisa took a long drag from her cigarette. "But that doesn't make me late."

"Fuck it don't," Woody answered.

"We ain't doin' shit till Sal gets here."

"You were supposed to have your bitch ass here a long time ago."

"We ain't doin shit 'til Sal gets here," Lisa reiterated.

They all looked across the table at each other. Lisa, Don, Woody, and Shorty. In the background during this exchange was Sal's wife Rachel, cleaning the kitchen and doing dishes. She was a quiet woman with short dark hair. She wore her usual t-shirt and cut-off shorts.

"When does Sal get home?" Shorty asked over his shoulder.

"Any time now," Rachel answered. "You want a beer?"

"But when does he get off work?" Woody asked.

"Half an hour ago," Rachel answered.

“Fucking late,” Woody said to Lisa. She ignored him and lit another cigarette.

“I’ll take a beer,” said Don.

Rachel pulled a cold bottle from the fridge and served it to Don.

“Well that’s the thing,” Woody started. “We got the bag here in front of us, and this broad bringing it late, and we have no word from the guy.”

“It don’t matter,” Shorty said. “Sal ain’t even home yet.

“Ya know,” Lisa said, “it’s fucking Sal who’s late, not me.”

“You were supposed to be here,” Woody complained.

“But I’m here now,” Lisa explained. “We’re waitin’ on Sal.”

“It happens,” Rachel said. “Sometimes he gets late tryin’ to leave the shop. Sometimes he stops for a beer.” Rachel went back to her cleaning. The kitchen really wasn’t that dirty. And she rarely paid this much attention to it. She was nervous though and needed something to do. She hoped Sal would come home soon. Really hoped, because she didn’t want to be left alone with these creeps. She didn’t want him skipping out on her when so much was at stake.

Sal made so many promises. Better things were going to happen after tonight. Her world was supposed to change. Just one night’s work with these thugs. These outlaws and bandits. Lowlifes, that is what Rachel called them. Especially that murderous bitch Lisa. She hated Lisa and was frightened every minute the woman was in the house. But after tonight they would live high on the hog. Move out of this trailer and get somewhere warm and tropical. Have a bungalow all to themselves and there would be no more Lisa or Shorty. They would all go their own ways after tonight. She would never see these people again, after tonight.

“But we got the fucking package,” Woody cried.

“The guy ain’t ready yet,” Lisa said.

"Why all the fucking secrecy?" Woody asked.

"Ain't no secret," Lisa said. "It's just a thing. Just the way it worked out. And I ain't late."

"The fuck you ain't," Woody said.

"Just shut the fuck up," Shorty said. "There's no reason for any of this shit. Let's just keep cool till Sal gets here."

"But the guy," Woody said.

"It's just a thing," Lisa answered.

"Your thing."

"You got that right."

"What the fuck is that supposed to mean?" Woody asked with increased irritation.

"Just what she fucking said!" shouted Don. "I'm getting sick of both of your shit. We gotta stick together on this."

"Don's right," said Shorty. "We gotta see it through. It's not just the guy, but the bosses too. They got their thing."

"And we got ours," cried Woody.

"And we got ours," repeated Shorty. "And ain't a thing we can do till it's all ready. And it ain't gonna be ready 'till Sal gets here."

"So where the fuck is Sal?" asked Woody.

Rachel wanted to cry. She wiped her face with dish water, hoping the moisture would cover her emotional state. She was thinking back to last night with Sal.

"Under the bed," Sal had instructed her. "It's under the bed. If shit gets bad; just in case."

"Oh Sal!" she had cried. "I don't think I can do that."

"You'll have to. It will be the only way. Don't hold back and don't hesitate. They won't with you, so you don't with them. Just keep pumpin' and start runnin'. Don't stop. If I can I'll meet you at the place."

"What do you mean if you can?" Rachel had asked in terror.

"I'll be okay," Sal had answered. "Nothing can go

wrong. It's all in the bag. But just in case, I'm telling you how you have to be with these cocksuckers. There is no negotiating and they ain't leaving quietly. Just remember, it's under the bed."

Rachel stood at the kitchen sink and closed her eyes. She saw her Sal's smiling face. Smiling at her. After tonight, she mouthed to herself. Under the bed she remembered. Under the bed.

"Hey Rachel," Lisa said over her shoulder, "I'll take a beer too."

Rachel went to the refrigerator and got a beer for Lisa. She was repulsed by the idea of serving a drink and being hospitable to someone she never would have normally allowed into the room. She walked to Lisa and set the cold bottle down in front of her. Lisa's hand shot out and wrapped around Rachel's hand still on the bottle. She clenched the hand against the bottle with a vise grip.

"Hope Sal didn't run into some emergency," Lisa said.

"He can handle himself," Rachel said as she jerked her hand away.

"I want a look," Woody said.

"No one looks at shit," Lisa ordered. "We ain't doin' shit 'till Sal gets home."

The phone rang. It was a wall mounted phone right above Shorty's head. He answered it.

"Ya," he said. He sat listening for a few minutes. "It's Sal," he finally announced. "There's been a change of plans."

Lisa jumped up from her seat. She grabbed the bag and shouted, "No there hasn't been any fucking change!"

Woody was up also and he pulled a pistol from his boot. He leaned across the table, pointed it at Lisa and shouted, "Put the motherfucking bag down now!"

Lisa reached inside of her coat and pulled out a nine

millimeter and pointed it at Shorty. "The thing is now. We do it tonight!"

"Put the bag down cunt or I'm blowin' you away!" Woody shouted.

Rachel silently slipped out of the kitchen without anyone noticing. "Under the bed" she mouthed to herself repeatedly as she walked down the hallway.

Don reached for Woody's hand and startled Woody. He reacted by pistol whipping Don until his limp body fell to the ground. When he raised his hand again to point the gun at Lisa it was dripping with Don's blood. She looked at him incredulously. Her mouth dropped open and she looked down at Don.

"You kill 'em?" she asked.

"Shut the fuck up and put the bag back down now!"

Shorty suddenly felt cold steel against the back of his neck. He turned slowly and was face to face with Rachel's shotgun. Rachel was on the other end staring up at him.

"You give me that fucking phone right now you son-of-a-bitch or I'm blowin' your head off," she ordered.

"No need to going off halfcocked now Rachel," Shorty said.

"You sayin' that to me?" she asked. "Look down on the floor next to ya. I think he was a partner just a few seconds ago."

"Now look Rachel. There's lots of people interested in this thing. Sal here on the phone has business. We got a guy to see."

"That's right," Woody agreed. "So let's get fucking blondie here to drop the bag."

"Gimme the goddamned phone Shorty!"

Lisa swung her arm around and pointed her gun at Woody. "Drop that now you piece of shit!"

"You drop the bag cunt!" Woody answered.

Rachel jabbed Shorty with the end of her barrel.

"I'll hang it up," Shorty threatened.

"Put the bag down!" Woody ordered.

"You drop that fucking piece!" Lisa counter demanded.

Outside, the squirrels continued their play. The sun was setting and it would soon be time to curl up and sleep. In the coming days the weather would become cooler. Soon the night air would be crisp and it would be time for the squirrels to bed down and stay warm. But for now they could play. Up and down the length of the tree and jumping from limb to limb.

The loud sound of guns being fired rang out. Then there was a silence after the sudden shock of the loud explosions of gunpowder. The silence was deathly calm. Then it was gone. The squirrels were startled and instinctively ran to the top of the tree. They looked about and saw nothing. Tested the air with their noses, and smelled nothing. They quickly forgot their fear and went back to playing in the muggy summer evening. The only sound came from the cars driving on the highway beyond the fence.

School Assignment

Iris sat on the park bench alone, her head bent resting on the knee of her crossed leg, snoring. Her arms crossed on her lap. Shoulder length dark hair fell loosely from her head, covering her face and knees. In her hand she held a brown paper grocery sack. She was asleep, tired from a long night of work. She felt burned out already at the young age of twenty seven.

"Wake up," a gruff voice insisted. It was Otten. Iris knew he would arrive after her. She lifted her head; dark eyes were sunken in her face, swollen and shadowed with too much mascara. She didn't smile.

"You're late."

"I'm on time. Kira is late."

"She better show," Iris warned.

"You did your part?" Otten asked.

"I've got it." Iris held up the crumpled paper bag. Everything Iris owned was crumpled. Her black winter coat was crumpled, her jeans were crumpled, and even her white Nikes looked a bit crumpled. Her apartment was a mess of such crumpled things, a manifestation of her crumpled life.

Otten sat down on her left. Leaned his back against the park bench and looked out at the lake. He folded his arms across his chest. His beige Carhartt jacket was zipped up to his neck. It was scuffed and dirty from wearing it at work. As were his brown steel-toed work boots. There were various on tears in his blue jean pants. He was Iris' elder at forty seven years of age. He looked older.

"You sure this is safe?" he asked.

"Safer than the city."

"The houses on the lake make me nervous."

"There not paying any attention."

"I don't feel good about it," he reiterated. "Eureka Lake. Who even knew?"

"My Dad took me fishing here when I was a kid."

"Really? Any good?"

"We always fished from this bench, facing north. Early in the morning they would bite. Channel cat. Not always so good though."

Otten said nothing, he stared at the water as it rolled passed them. The chilly autumn breeze stirring up the chop. Iris looked around nervously.

"She better show soon."

"Don't worry about her," Otten said. "She'll find her way. It's not so easy for her to get around. Probably had to borrow some wheels."

"That's comforting."

"We're safe way out here," Otten concluded. "Hey, how about a peak in that bag."

"Not yet."

"I just want to see it."

"Wait for Kira."

"I don't see what would be wrong with a little peek."

"We ain't doing anything yet. No peeking. No talking. No deal until I get the call." Iris pulled a cell phone from the jacket of her pocket and set it on her knee. She clutched the paper bag a bit tighter.

"No problem," Otten reassured. "I just wanted a peek was all. I don't really care, as long as I get paid."

"No one gets paid; no one gets nothin', until the phone rings."

"I'm getting paid. After what I went through last night, I'm g'tting' paid. Today."

"Well don't look at me. We gotta wait for Kira."

"And the phone call."

"The whole deal depends on the phone call."

Otten continued to stare at the lake. The movement of the water was relaxing. Any other time it would lull him to sleep. Any time other than this morning. Iris glanced at his shaved head and noticed how round it was. His blonde eyebrows were hard to see against his fair skin. His blue eyes were mean. Otten worked too much, too hard, day after day. And he worked hard on this deal. The work made his eyes mean with an attitude of distrust. There was much Otten didn't understand about the world. His ignorance made him afraid, which made him suspicious.

"I finally found the party," came a voice from behind the two. It was Kira, flashing a huge smile. Bright eyed and bushy tailed. Her black skin glistening in the September sun. She hadn't put in the leg work the other two had, but her important task was today. She carried a small green backpack that was of particular interest to the other two. She sat herself down without pomp on the other side of Iris. Her tiny boyish legs didn't touch the ground. She laughed out loud at the sight of the two on the bench. Her mouth opened wide with her laughter, exposing a gold stud through the end of her tongue. She was the perky baby of the group at age twenty.

"What's so fucking funny?" Iris asked.

"You two are so pathetic looking. Rough night?"

"Haven't been to sleep yet," grumbled Otten.

"So why didn't we do this tonight?"

"The deal is almost done," Iris explained. "Just a phone call away and it's over. No one is around early. I feel safe here early."

"You should," Kira agreed. "It's far enough away from town that's for sure." She zipped her black leather jacket up to her neck and hugged herself to try to stay warm. "Hey Iris, how about a peek."

"No peeking," Otten explained. "No deal, no nothin' until she gets the phone call."

Iris tapped the phone resting on her knee.

"That thing got juice to it?" Kira asked.

Iris' eyes opened a little wider at the thought. She quickly snatched up the phone and opened it to check. "Plenty enough for our purposes," she answered.

"I thought you wouldn't own a phone?"

"The guy gave it to me. Said not to do nothing without the phone call"

"So here we sit," Otten explained. He rolled his eyes. Kira smirked, the two gold piercings in her lower lip sparkled in the sun's reflection off the water.

"Just doin' what I was told," Iris explained.

"The thing is done," Otten complained. "Just give me my cut so I can go."

Iris held the bag up so both could see. "You want this Otten? You want to deliver this fucking thing? Do you know what to do with it? Do you know the deal?"

"I don't care so much about the deal with no sleep." He pulled a silver flask from the pocket of the Carhartt, unscrewed the top, and took a long swig. Iris sat the bag back into her lap and looked at Kira, who said nothing. Gave her best poker face.

"So what do you think of it?" Kira asked nodding toward the bag.

"The bag?" Iris countered. I don't know."

"What do you mean you don't know? You know something that we don't."

"I haven't looked."

"You've been carrying that around with you and you haven't looked?"

"I was told not to…"

"So what?" Otten asked. "You have it, you have to look."

"I'm a professional. I was told not to look, so I didn't look."

"You're lying," Kira accused.

"What if it is something I'm not supposed to see? What if they kill me for it?"

"Who the hell are they?" Otten asked.

"The ones who are going to call. The ones who made this deal. And the deal is to not look in the damn bag."

"Well they," Otten started, "are going to assume that you looked. What then?"

"They know of me. They know I'm a professional and I will do as I'm told."

Otten shook his head. "So what's in the backpack?"

"I don't know," Kira answered.

"You've got to be kiddin' me!" Otten exclaimed. "Neither of you know what you are carrying? Neither of you know what the hell is going on? Shit, I probably know more about this deal than either of you. I worked my ass off last night for this shit. What are you guys, just mules?"

There was a long quiet pause while the three reflected on the dawn's events. The morning was becoming warmer, the sun was rising higher in the sky. People were starting to leave their homes. An old plump man arrived across the lake and started to fish.

"I'm nervous," Otten proclaimed.

"Get ahold of yourself," Kira demanded.

"We're in a bad spot."

"For what?" Iris asked. "A drive by?"

"It's getting to active around here."

"He's right," Kira said. "Check the phone again."

Iris flipped the phone open and studied it. "Damn."

"What is it?" Kira asked.

Iris held the phone up above her head and stared at it. "No signal."

"Okay!" Otten stammered. "Okay…"

"We have to move," Kira said. "Back to town."

"No one is going anywhere," Iris barked. "That's trouble. So it's my fault for picking this park. I thought it would be safe. If we leave now we jeopardize the deal."

"Kira is right," Otten said. "We need to move back to town."

"That's a bad idea. No one leaves."

They fell silent for a few reflective moments. The water from the lake was still choppy. They could smell the autumn blowing through the trees. Iris looked at the phone again. She had reception for a minute and then she didn't.

"Shit," she cursed. "They might have called, they might not have."

"Getting reception?" Kira asked.

"Intermediate."

"Well the way I figure it," Otten started, "one of these bags has our money…"

"And one has fuck-all who cares," Iris interjected.

Otten was warming up from the sun, he unzipped his Carhartt. Iris saw blood stains on his t-shirt. She said nothing but felt a chill run down her spine.

"The bag has money in it," Iris explained.

"You said you didn't know!" Otten said passionately.

"I lied."

"So what?" Kira asked. "A three way split?"

"I dunno. I'm not the one with blood on my shirt."

Kira bent forward for a better look at Otten. Her smile had long disappeared. She decided she too was getting warm and removed her leather jacket. She covered the back pack with it on her lap. Her white sleeveless t-shirt was clean. Dark tattoos showed on her arms and shoulders. Some of them words, some pictures.

"Let's count it," Otten offered. "Maybe a three way split is good enough."

"There's seventy five thousand." Iris replied.

“Well aren’t you just the nosey little shit.”

“You want me to look and not count?”

“Cheeky,” Otten said. “I’m happy with twenty five.” He was looking around the park, his blue eyes darting about anxiously. People were walking dogs, joggers were appearing. More came to fish the lake. He took another swallow from the flask.

Kira lifted her jacket. “That leaves me holding the bag.”

“We have to look,” Otten instructed. Iris said nothing. She was no longer calling the shots. The three were a collective. Bound by the dilemma they found themselves in. “We have to know what we are dealing with.”

“Divide up the money first,” Kira said. “Then we open this bag. Otten is right; we have to see what is in here.”

Iris silently counted out twenty-five thousand dollars for each of them. She was nervous also. Her dark brooding eyes had an earnestness to them as she counted. She kept looking about the park to see if they were being watched.

Kira stood, laid her jacket on the bench, moved to a position in front of the other two and knelt on the ground. Like ripping off a band aid she unzipped the green backpack. With both hands she opened the flap. They took a collective deep breath and bent to look into the bag.

“Oh my!” Kira exclaimed.

“Damit!” Otten cursed.

“I knew it,” Iris said softly. “I knew this deal was trouble.”

Suddenly the phone rang.

Three Days

Part two of *The Transgressive Therapist*

They didn't speak again until cresting the top of the bridge. The confusion of the accident scene was cooled by the time they arrived and people were gathering around each other while others worked intently to keep the traffic moving. The women with her two children were standing alongside their vehicle. She held the hand of the small child, who was holding the hand of her older sister. The woman looked as though she had been crying the entire time. She had a blanket from some caring EMT wrapped around her, and she dotted her eyes with the corner of it. The children looked about with lost eyes, holding tight to each other…

"I gotta ditch this van," she was saying, her voice piercing Casey's dream state. Like a knife through the dark, exposing the waking world as well as all of the aches and pains from the past freezing evening.

"Will I see you again?" Casey asked.

"It's up to you," Alex responded. "Come by anytime. I live straight back a couple miles on the road in a log cabin, the only one.

"This is the Higgs home. You don't need to talk to Higgs though. Karen will be there. I've packed you a duffle with some of my cold weather gear, and anything else you might need. Karen will ask you for items. They are in the duffle. Give them to her when she asks."

"What are the items?"

"Do you remember last night at all?"

"It's fuzzy. I was asleep."

"Not all the time. You're dead though, remember. You need to keep moving. Karen and I have a standing arrangement for getting people to safe places."

"Dead people?"

"Out Casey. I gotta fly." She reached across his lap and opened the door for him to exit. He stood in the snow and watched her turn the van around and sped off.

"But you said you wouldn't dump me," Casey said quietly to the van as it faded into the distance.

Boson Higgs lives in a rusty doublewide at the back end of a dismal lonely manufactured home park so close to the northern border it can be hard to distinguish the small trailer gathering as Canadian or the State of 10,000 Lakes. The inside of the trailer is just as bleak as the outside.

The smelly obese Higgs enjoys communicating electronically. One of Boson's four computers is used solely for the purpose of operating a ham radio and antenna set up. Next to that computer is a citizen band radio, which Boson is more active with than anything else in his shrine to electronics. Dressed only in bib overalls the red-faced man slides back and forth on his bench, which spans the length of the shrine. Probably the most exercise he performs during the day. From chat rooms, chess games, and radios he slides, all the while listening to the thirteen-inch television. Boson listened to CNN and glanced from time to time to read the news ticker at the bottom of the screen. He drinks diet colas and smokes Camels nonstop in a masterful display of multitasking ability.

This is how Casey found Boson Higgs and Karen. He couldn't figure out the relationship between Karen and Boson. She didn't seem happy to be in residence of Higgs' trailer, so he assumed some kind of blood relation. She was close to Casey's age, and Higgs had at least twenty years on them both. Her dark hair was long and her dark eyes alert. She looked like a thoughtful person who didn't smile much. He imagined she would be much more attractive if she would smile more often.

"Codependency is bullshit," Karen said from the kitchen. This is how Casey got to know her, during the explanation of her family philosophy. "I'm a creator. I created that fat bastard. He was completely different when we met. Now look at him. I gave him those addictions. I keep reinforcing his life style. Cook for him, clean, shop. This is my doing. He is a puppet and I play with him as I please."

"You're a raving lunatic!" Higgs shouted over the TV. "And you, friend of Alex. Wonder what she saw in you."

Higgs was turned on his bench to see the newly formed duo. His voice was deep and sounded irritated. Casey didn't care. He saw the sofa Higgs slept on across the room, figuring the old man moved from the bench to the couch, and that was about it. So out of shape and flabby was this man, with a long gray beard growing down to his potbelly. His bark was definitely worse than any bite he could have.

Casey watched as Higgs lit a cigarette, coughed, wheezed, and took another drag. "That's my Karen you're leaving with. She's taking you to the end of the road pal. Life gets tricky when you run out of road."

"Got any advice old timer?" Casey asked.

"Yeah, do everything the little girl says to do. She knows what and who is out there when it gets dark. She knows where she is and what needs to be done. Do everything she tells you to do without fail, then you'll be fine." Higgs took another drag from his cigarette, coughed, and turned to his radio.

"You're Karen," Casey stated, turning in her direction at the kitchen table.

"In the flesh," Karen responded. "Did Alex pack you a bag?"

Casey held the bag up for her to see.

"In the back mister. We go by snowmobile from here.

It's going to take the rest of the day to travel to the river. Let's grab a meal before we leave."

The river is a dark wild mystery, loud but invisible under the blanket of darkness. The night is overcast and no stars are reflected in the rough waters, or ghostly reflection of the moon. The sound of rushing water is eerie in the darkness. An unforeseen threat ready to trip a person up and push them downstream among the lethal rocks ahead. A phenomenon sounding so lonely as to remind Casey of the rickety sound of a train riding the rails he was accustomed to from his youth.

Gehenna sat still and studied Sarah, a petite blond woman no bigger than herself. Unhappy; she could tell right away. Sarah sat still and quiet, like it might be a competition. It made Gehenna feel uncomfortable.

"So what's with the bird tattoos," Sarah observed. "Those are tattoos right?"

"They're from an old poem," Gehenna replied. She wasn't about to throw her pearls before the swine…

"Did Casey know?"

This was a hint of what Casey sometimes alluded to in past sessions, competition and childishness. Did Casey know indeed? Casey knew enough for their relationship almost to be an affair of sorts. Unprofessional on her part, she gave too much to him.

"There are a lot more of those people lately," Sarah observed.

"People like who?" Gehenna asked.

"You know what I mean. Mental."

"That's not a real nice thing to say," Gehenna said.

"It's what they say in other countries."

"It's disrespectful,"

"Well there are more, seems like more and more than usual."

"Maybe it's always been like this," Gehenna said. "Maybe mental illness has always affected the same percentage of people all through time. We have the Internet now, the media, and hundreds of movies about crazy people."

"What would you think if that wasn't true," Sarah pointed out. "Half of my friends are on antidepressants. Most of my friends I've known since grade school. They never seemed crazy before. Something happened when they grew older."

"They weren't crazy? I remember young people acting insane, girls getting murdered in cars, guys shooting each other over a bag of weed, kids overdosing in school.

"But for the sake of argument, let's expand on this paranoid delusion of yours."

"What does that mean?" she had a fading smile, "Gehenna? Did I pronounce it correct?"

"It means Casey is dead. Case closed. I've closed the file and stored it in my drawer. It means I don't have to talk about Casey again. I don't have to think about him ever again. I can concentrate on my other clients, the ones with insurance coverage. "Are you paying cash on your way out? We're into this for twenty minutes. You plan on staying and pay the rest of the hour on your way out?"

"I don't really care about your wife," Karen said blandly.

"Give me the weed."

"What weed?" Casey asked.

"The weed Alex gave you. She gave you weed for payment."

"Payment?"

"I need to be paid," Karen explained. "I can't be expected to take you all the way to the river, cross on the ferry, and take you north for free."

"Makes sense," Casey agreed. He reached into his parka and produced the bag of pot Alex gave him. Karen took it from his hands and stuffed it into her snow-covered duffle. She turned to examine the river, looked back at Casey with a distressed look on her face.

"The water is really moving," she said. "We can't cross yet, too rough and dangerous."

Casey looked through the heavy snowfall. He could hardly see the fast moving water in the darkness. Karen removed the tarp from her duffle. "Let's cover up," she suggested.

"We're waiting it out?" Casey asked.

"Probably till morning."

"We're spending the night under the tarp?"

"All nice and cozy," Karen smiled sarcastically. "And we're smoking dope too." She sat on the wooden planks of the ferry, cold and wet from the snow. She covered up and held a corner of the tarp for Casey to enter. He sat next to her.

"See," she said. "All comfy." Karen retrieved the bag of pot from her duffle along with a metal pipe to smoke with.

"That's just like the one I had in high school," Casey said.

"Best for traveling, she pointed out. Glass breaks." Karen filled the pipe and held it by the wooden stem to light it.

"Do you believe in God?" Casey asked.

"Nope," Karen answered.

"I do. It explains all of this."

"All of what? Wet, cold, slushy snow?"

"That and the mountains, trees…"

"Butterflies and squirrels?" Karen asked sardonically.

"So what do you believe in?"

"I have a list," Karen said.

"Do tell," Casey urged.

"Love, law, will, knowledge, wisdom."

"Love is first eh?"

"Of course," Karen answered. She hesitated thoughtfully. "It's all about love."

"Even if there is no God?"

"Oh there's a God," Karen explained. "I just don't believe in Him. I believe in the list."

Casey started buzzing from the weed. He fell silent, as he always had in the past. Pot caused him to retreat into himself more than usual, and this time was no exception. There was little light from down the road; he couldn't make out what it was from. The light cast a seductive shadow through the falling snow, tree branches holding snow by the arm-full. The shapes took on a human quality and were animated by the blowing breeze.

He could trace the lines with his eyes. Different shapes and sizes, round and thin, tall giants. And Alex. He found Alex through the wind and snow. Saw her lines take shape in the dark, her supple curves, the back of her neck. Casey closed his eyes and he could feel her arms around him, her breath on his neck.

Waiting for the candlelight to fade, anticipating the rise of the morning star, a cold, quiet blanket of snow covers everything, has everyone asleep. Alex is alone in the dark twirling and spinning slowly, her thin skirt swirls loosely around her short legs, drops down around her ankles.

She dances in her own world. A drug dance sparkles in her eyes, deep set in black mascara. She is not there, and then she is back again. In and out, like a visitor. Always dancing to the music slowly. Perfect for her waking dream.

"She fucked you!" Karen's voice shocked Casey from his reverie.

"What?" He answered.

"Ah!" she shouted. "She fucked you. I can't believe it."

"What are you so upset about?"

"I'm not upset!"

"You're shouting."

"Alex never has sex. I can't believe she would seduce you and then send you to me."

"What do you have to do with it?" Casey was confused.

"I get you over the river is all. Once you get across you won't come back. Alex should only screw people who stay."

Casey was silent. He didn't know what Karen was talking about. During the silence her eyes became heavy and she yawned. The silence persisted as she lay back on the cold wood and fell asleep. Casey did the same, falling asleep amidst his mental muddiness.

"Wake up!" Karen shouted in Casey's face. He awoke startled and disoriented.

"Don't just lay there and look at me like that," Karen demanded. She was busy packing up gear from last night. Filling both of their duffels. "The temperature went up at least thirty degrees overnight, all the snow is melting and creating fog. Real fog Casey, thick as chowder."

Casey stood on tired wobbly legs. "I need more sleep," he announced.

"No time. Chop chop Casey! If we go now we can maybe sneak by the toll master."

"I don't get it," Casey said while rubbing the sleep from his eyes.

Karen continued to pack until she zipped the duffels. "You got any cash?" She asked." I need cash to get into the city. I can't buy my way in with pot Casey. The toll masters can't go to their boss with a bag of pot. Only cash."

"Sounds dangerous," Casey said.

Karen stared at him blankly.

"It's the principle I guess. The fucking toll masters are a bunch of thugs and I'm a scofflaw."

"Are any of the women up here law abiding citizens?" Karen ignored him.

Casey looked out over the river in the dark of night. It was an entirely different beast in the night. Invisible, almost sinister, ready to gobble people and send them into oblivion.

"Or," she sighed, "we can go back. Your choice."

"Really?" Casey asked sardonically.

The line for the ferry snapped with a loud pop. Rushing currents of fast moving energy yanked Karen into the river on the loose ferry. Her eyes wide with surprise for only a moment. Casey watched as she knelt next to her bag and loaded her shotgun. She fades into the darkness of the river as the ferry is pulled farther from shore.

"Ride the snowmobile back!" Karen shouts. "Stick to the wet muddy trail! Go now!"

Casey stood at the shore dumbfounded. A shot suddenly rang out. He couldn't move. His legs were glued to the shoreline. Another shot rings out. Then another. In the flash Casey can see Karen's silhouette. She looked determined. Another shot rang out from the river, and something whizzed past Casey's left ear. He dropped to the ground. After moments of silence he stood on all fours and crawled to his snowmobile. Five shots in succession broke the silence. Casey didn't even look back. If she doesn't know what she was getting into, then she's dead. If she has control of the situation he may see her again. But for now all he could think of is starting the snowmobile and getting the hell away from here.

The ride through the mud was maddening. Casey wasn't familiar with snowmobiles in snow, much less on mud. He envisioned Karen dead along the riverbank and some faceless toll master on her snowmobile chasing after him. Throwing caution to the wind he throttled the machine, avoiding tree limbs and rocks, the mud splattered behind him splashing his coat and covering him with the cold moist clay.

The sky was graying and snow started to fall again He didn't know what this would mean for his ride. It seemed as though he had been driving for a long time, longer than it took them to get to the river. He didn't see the mobile home park, so he pressed on. He knew eventually the road would end at Alex's cabin. All the while he waited for the sound of gunfire from behind. He raced ahead trying to stay on the road, fighting the machine in the mud, and now the snow. The trip seemed to take hours, and then the snowmobile stopped running. Probably out of gas.

Casey was frustrated and exhausted. The sun was rising and the snow still falling. He kicked at the dead snowmobile. This was going to be a tough day. The snowmobile was pointed in the right direction, but he knew if he continued on foot the trail would lead him off his course. It could be the end of him.

"What am I doing?" he asked into the wind blown pink sky. "How did I let myself wind up here?"

"Talking to yourself is the first sign of snow madness," a voice said from the dark wilderness.

"I've never heard of snow madness," Casey answered.

A silhouette emerged from the tree line. "That's because I made it up," the shadow said. It was Alex.

"I thought I would never see you again," he said.

"Heading for the cabin?"

"Trying to."

"Well you pretty much made it. It's just around the curve."

"Oh good," Casey said sardonically. "Are you coming or going?"

"Going. But you're welcome to let yourself in."

"Where are you off to?"

"Got some errands to run. Need a car."

"Where is your van?" Casey asked. He was starting to shiver, the morning turning colder.

"I ditched the van so I need a new vehicle."

"Why?" He asked.

"It was stolen Casey!"

"Where will you find a new one?"

"Where do you think?" She answered with a roguish smile on her face. "Come on. Soon it will be your third day of death. I said I wouldn't dump you."

Ghost Sickness

> *"Preoccupation with death and the deceased. Various symptoms possible: bad dreams, weakness, feelings of danger, loss of appetite, fainting, dizziness, fear, anxiety, hallucinations, loss of consciousness, confusion, feelings of futility, and a sense of suffocation." – DSM IV*

While dancing, young Ivy watches herself in the smoky dark mirrors that make up the south wall of the large night club. She should be working the small crowd surrounding the dance floor but she captivates herself; loves her tight fitting costume that she put together herself. Her farmer's daughter look with cornflower blue cut off Daisy Dukes and ankle high cowboy boots. That's all that would matter, because the red flannel shirt would be off in another minute or so. As soon as the dollar bills started showing, then she would stop watching herself dance and work the crowd. Stop watching as her auburn hair tossed down around her back. Stop checking her technique at the pole.

The river shore was Zach's brooding haunt. It was a place of reverie, a port marking the continuation of life, a berth marking the death of love. Zach sat on the river's edge contemplating life, and death. He was missing his friend this morning. A friend of long ago and long gone. Things would be different if she were here now. He always thought that. Especially at the river's edge and especially when things weren't going his way. The river washed away the bad feelings if he sat there long enough. He loved when the weather was rough and the river was alive with chop. It seemed the harder he looked at the waves the more of his troubles were washed away with the cold, dark, polluted city water.

Lucky people received grief counseling. Lucky people had a therapist to work things out with. And even luckier people had a good therapist to work things out with. All Zach had was the river. When times were tough he spent a lot of time on the smelly shore watching the water float by. Sometimes he fished the waters, just to stay longer. As if he really needed an excuse. There was no one at home to make excuses to. He lived by himself, alone. But sitting in the car was boring some days. This morning it was all he had, he needed to be at work soon. He wasn't exactly washed clean, but he was well enough for the day's labor.

"So what?" he asked aloud as he steered his old beaten up Escort back onto the freeway toward work. "People die every day."

Zach knew about the whole thing. He was there when she told him so he was there to observe which makes it real. It became real when her body was found and her face was puffed up and blue. But no one knew that the entirety of the event was witnessed before. As explained by her, Iris, to his face as they shared a cake and coffee, smoked cigarettes and watched television. That was when she blurted it out.

"I'm going to hang myself right there in the closet." This was observed after the fact and talked about at the funeral. The words passed on from one observer to the other until it reached his ear and then he knew her to be true to her word, that the closet was the place. So no one knew except Iris and Zach that the thing was played out ahead of time, step by step, while the joint was still burning and during the commercials, this was how it was going to happen. So it was real from that point on.

Did Iris really kill herself? Did she take her own life alone in such a horrible darkness? Who was there to observe, over fifteen years ago? Who made it real? It was the most real for Zach because he was there to witness the before and the after like no one else had. But no one was there when Iris was alone, in the dark with nothing but the belt. No whiskey to drink or pills to take, just the pain and the alone; just her. So did it really happen? That is why funerals are so important. Why it is necessary to view the body.

But no one was there to observe Iris at her moment of courage. Sometimes it takes years of practice to perform that one final misstep into the unknown void. And as she was the only witness then it was nothing and it never happened. Only the darkness happened. No pact in the world could make that a reality. Make it into something that it was not. She alone observed her last breath though she was probably unconscious by that time, which made the event even more of a non-happening.

Still, in the end, Iris was no more. The magic of the mortician is never enough to bring that last breath into reality. Left to her own devices Iris had a fifty percent chance of surviving on her own; of leaving that tiny apartment alive to walk again into the cold night of winter having a cigarette and a drink of whiskey.

In Zach's limited understanding the thing just didn't happen. The mortician did his best but there she lay as alone as she was that night when she said her last words, and breathed her last breath. That was the thing of it that never happened. That was the basis of Zach's confusion.

There were two types of dancers, those who were just working and those who were turned on. Ivy was of the latter. Those dancers who were turned on had short nights compared to those who were just going through the motions. But she was a professional too. She never let her orgasms show. And most nights she lost track of how many she had. It was those private dances with the private parts.

She had a way of closing in on a guy, or a gal. She liked either one, because she could melt them both.

Part of Ivy's thing was to pretend to kiss the client. She tried to see how close she could bring her lips to the client without actually kissing them, the sweet breath of her mouth caressing a chin, or a cheek. This was how she really made her money. She could feel the hardness of her male clients while she gyrated on their laps, completely naked with the hardness trying to penetrate her through the clothing. Her lips spread and ready to engulf. This is when she became all squishy herself, especially for her regulars. This was when she came, and how she made the real money.

Sometimes they came too, even the girls. None could resist. And who didn't like a pretty girl, naked on their lap, thrust and grinding against them. Another thing that was part of Ivy's repertoire was gliding down between the clients legs with the length of her supple body. Her face between their thighs wishing they were naked too. That was when she most often had an orgasm herself. She wished at times that she could touch herself, but that would be unprofessional. Instead she used her mouth to do more than tease. The days of the strip tease were over. Now were the days of the strip please. There was little talk among the other dancers of this. Orgasms may be discussed, but not the sex. Because that is what it was after all. Even though the pants were on she still took what was engorged into her mouth and tried to go as deep as a pair of jeans would allow.

Ivy did not understand those who were just trying to get through the shift. That would drive her insane. It wasn't like she was a sex addict. She didn't even have a partner. She hadn't had any real intimacy in years, and she existed just fine without. She was too busy with little Della anyways. A child can take a lot out of a person by the end of the day.

It being before the internet meant that somebody told Iris

these things. You don't just tie a belt around your neck without some kind of idea of what you are doing. It's a difficult thing to do and only now with the use of the information superhighway is it possible to read studies and police reports about others who have gone before. There are books with step by step instructions on how to hang oneself. There are websites, newsgroups, and online communities devoted to this subject. Does the buckle lie in front or the back of the neck? You gotta do it right so that unconsciousness settles in. Otherwise a person is just left to be strangled while awake, a special kind of hell.

Suicide by hanging does not really involve a snap of the neck. The idea is to cut off the blood flow to the brain, usually with the knot of the rope on the left side so the correct arteries are pinch closed. The snapping of the neck came about with public hangings. It was to disgusting to just strangle somebody in front of a crowd. What with all of the kicking and flailing about. So the drop was used to snap the neck causing paralysis. This way the crowd assumed the guilty party to be dead when really they are being strangled to death, which could take up to twenty minutes to achieve the final outcome. Hopefully the hanged person is unconsciousness and does not have to endure the nightmare of being strangled to death. But at least that is what seems to happen in every case of self-strangulation. The body goes unconscious and then the brain dies.

This is what Iris achieved. This was why her face was so bloated and blue. And this is what was discussed, probably with a new found friend at one of the many institutions Iris frequented. She had been sent all over the state through the years, from psyche ward to psyche ward as doctors wanted a crack at her to see if they could extract a cure.

"It's settled then," Iris said to some unnamed face in an

unimaginable place. "We have a pact. Do it before we reach thirty. Neither of us will see the age of thirty."

Zach stood at the precipice ready to take the leap with cover charge in hand and whiskey on his breath, hoping to find her, the link to his past. He nervously adjusted his tie. He looked better than the usual dirt bags that frequented the club. "A gentlemen's club," he muttered under his breath. He knew that he was probably the only gentleman there that night. He was dressed well. Better than the other patrons, better than the bouncers, better than the host taking the cover charge from his hand.

He placed himself at the end of the runway. Along the stage the dirt bags lined up. Drinking and carrying on belligerently. He waited patiently for Ivy. He waited to see her beautiful young naked body.

When Ivy stopped looking in the mirrors she would have to start working. She could read the small group of dull eyed men like an instruction manual. Insert peg A into slot B. That one right there, he was turned on. The others were not as motivated as this one. She named him Buck because the man looked like her cousin Buck back in Tennessee. Buck was good for a lap dance. The suit and tie at the end of the runway might want more than a lap dance. He might part with a hundred dollars, or even more. He was bright eyed and wouldn't take his gaze off of her. He wasn't drinking. Good. She grew so tired of the stinking alcohol breath by the end of the night. And sober men, they wanted more. Looking wasn't enough. This one had some cash and he would be willing to part with some of it.

Again, the technique was important; different from her talent at the pole, but the same thing really. Voluptuous seduction, in its many forms, meant rent money. That is what she considered sometimes, as she looked into the dark mirrors. At those times she wasn't watching herself dance.

She was adding and subtracting. Trying to think of how much she needed to make the rent that month. The shirt and tie at the end of the runway just might balance the books. She approached him, naked, showing off the one tattoo on her hip; the name of her mother inked in black, Iris.

Bonz the Femnazi Doll Face Babe

On either end of a long block of bridge expanse were traffic lights that seemed to be timed in a sequence customized with the single intent of frustrating one woman. She sat in her Volkswagen Bug at the intersection of Hamilton and Fayette considering this very thing for about the fifteenth time this weekend.

Bonz knew that she was going to try it again. She stepped on the clutch and let the small vehicle roll toward the intersecting street when she noticed the opposite street light change to yellow.

The light at the next intersection was already green, and at normal speed it would be red by the time she crossed the bridge. That was the challenge, to beat the timing and hit the intersection while the light was still green, with the Bug.

The light changed to green and she stepped on the gas. The little Volkswagen groaned a complaint and coughed a little smoke as Bonz pushed the pedal to the floorboard. Her timing with the clutch and gear shift were not good enough to gain enough speed. The light was red by the time the Bug crossed the bridge expanse.

"Figures," she said to herself. "Came up short again."

After saying this aloud she reached for her wrist and tugged on the rubber band worn there. Bonz did as her therapist had instructed and stretched the rubber band slightly before letting it go with a snap. This was meant as a self-inflicted punishment for every negative thing she would say about herself.

She contemplated the legitimacy of this practice until the light changed green and she moved the little vehicle off the bridge. The Bonz lit a cigarette as she drove. Home was her destination, a place where she cared for her three children, alone. The eldest of the three being a teenage girl who was watching the younger boys while Bonz had been in school that morning studying for her sociology degree.

She kept an eye on the rear view mirror as she neared the house. Just as the police had instructed her to do. "Always be aware of your surroundings," they had warned.

"The stats," she thought to herself. Macro sociology always had her looking at the big picture. The statistics showed that a stalker never stopped until the inevitable outcome was achieved. The murder of the victim.

The week before she had to explain to the grade school authorities that her boys did not know their home phone number because she could not teach it to them. Fear of phone harassment was just one of many symptoms of the lifestyle she was forced to live. He will still get the number though. He always does, one way or another. A stalker's talents are numerous.

Any inch will give him a mile. A phone number would mean endless hours of harassment. Without the order of protection he would be constantly badgering her, always with the threat of more physical violence. Still she wondered when it would come. When would he barge in on her class to "have it out with her"? Or maybe at the grocery store, movie theater, a friend's house. What friends though. Bonz kept very few. She was too afraid of that scenario.

The Bonz parked her Bug on the street and was careful not to mace herself as she searched for the house key. She unlocked the door and glanced over her shoulder one last time before entering her home. Was he out there now? Watching? Waiting?

"Somehow," she thought to herself, "I expected my marriage to be different from this. And the divorce to be civil."

"Do you write e-mail to your ex-wife?"

"Yes I do."

"When was the last time you wrote a letter to her?"

"It's been a couple of weeks."

The lawyer stood and presented her new evidence to the judge, and then to the witness.

"Did you write this letter?"

"Yes I did," his voice cracked.

"Did you write this letter that states that you do not understand the divorce decree, but that your lawyer advised you that the defendant had responsibility for all of the bills?"

"Yes!" he shouted before jumping from the stand and running to his lawyer's bench.

"I have no questions," the attorney for the plaintiff said with a chuckle.

After, we found ourselves in the courtyard engaged in post court smoking. The day was overcast and cool. A breeze was picking up, carrying the promise of rain in its path.

"He did not look good," the Bonz observed. "He looked like he had been drinking again."

"He looked like a beaten dog," I added. "No curses this time. I assumed he was going to condemn me to hell in front of the judge. Did you see him jump from the stand? He didn't even give his own lawyer a chance to cross examine."

"He thought he was going to get busted for breaking the order of protection. You know he's not to harass you electronically anymore," the lawyer explained.

"I have no idea what just happened," I confessed.

"We won!" she said with a smile.

"We did?" the Bonz asked excitedly.

"The judge said that due to the evidence, especially the e-mail, it was clear that neither party understood the decree. Therefore it was void."

"You mean I'm not divorced?"

"Technically you are. What we have to do is vacate the order. We'll be starting from scratch. I have never heard of such a thing in divorce proceedings," she sounded so proud of herself.

"I had no idea that was happening," Bonz said.

"I was no help," said the lawyer. "I had to write down everything the judge was saying. He was giving me instructions on how to vacate the order. Always remember, if you see a lawyer writing in court, that lawyer is winning."

Button Down Howard

Howard only wears button down white shirts $22.95 a piece at Sears. Buys them individually wrapped in plastic packaging with cardboard in the collar. Black slacks and matching socks. Keeps a pack of Pall Malls in his breast pocket and never uses a pocket protector. Drives a Buick and trades it in every three years. His home is on the edge of town, though he grew up closer to the heart of the city, which is now a run-down crime ridden area his mother refuses to leave because it was nice when she moved there and it's all she knows. His two story McMansion is one of many cookie cutter structures in a neighborhood run by a council of homeowners who all agreed on artificial turf instead of lawns.

He drinks black coffee but never had an espresso. His life is filled with "have nevers". The woman he married, and Howard, "have never" taken a vacation together. They "have never" paid more than twenty dollars for a bottle of wine. "Have never" dined out anywhere but a buffet. "Have never" had sex more than twice a month. "Have never" watched a movie together. "Have never" had a fight, or a kind word.

Howard is depressed but doesn't know it. Assumes everyone feels the same, and spends his days trying to rationalize the dualities he is certain governs the laws of his universe. Like how he feels ashamed that his favorite actress is Mia Kirshner, but has never tasted the vodka-besotted lips of a stranger at two in the morning.

The grimy window to his air-conditioned office looks out over the shop. Howard can see the workers all day, and they can see him. He seldom walks the wooden steps down to the shop floor because it can reach one hundred and twenty degrees down there; the workers are sweaty, tired, and mostly embittered. He knows this because he was down there for the larger part of his career, looking up at the prick in the window having an easy day in the coolness, going over green ledgers on a dusty computer monitor, and reading the newspaper at lunch.

Two fingers on each of Howard's hands are permanently turned inward from endlessly grinding small flame cut flanges on a noisy disk sander. Most of the nerve endings in his thumb are dead from nibbling burrs off larger pieces of metal. He can still taste the grit in his mouth. The production halls are poorly lit and resemble a cave filled with dead air that has never seen sunshine or felt rain.

Each day he remembers the voluptuous blonde girlfriend from his youth, his best buddy who moved across the state, the Christmas of his youth and the red Schwinn with a banana seat, and when Howard's father said "I love you", the day he passed away.

Death Dance

There is little I can say I hate. But I dislike carrying in groceries. My apartment is on the second floor, where I live alone. Two paper bags full are all I can manage. A bit of a struggle as I maneuver them from my car into my arms. Out of the corner of my eye I see the cemetery. It borders the backyard of the apartment building.

Another struggle to retrieve the keys from the pocket of my jeans, unlock and open the door to the building, make my way upstairs, unlock and open my apartment. Then I have a little rest before unpacking the grocery bags. Rib eye steaks, French fries, sausage, eggs, and a six-pack of Peroni.

One steak stays out while I put the rest of the groceries away. Grab the charcoal briquettes and head for the balcony to fire up the grill. The smoke spirals up into the cool night air like a prayer to the Gods. The smell is amazing. As I flip red meat on my grill, I look out at the cemetery. The sun set is sometimes heavy over the graves. It carries the weight of a solemn blanket, covering those who sleep. I don't think too much of my own mortality, and make a silent toast to youth before drinking a gulp of Peroni. Then another toast, to being alone.

I live alone and prefer it. Sometimes it can be hard to explain to people how "alone" is my chosen lifestyle. Most of my friends spend a great deal of time trying to not be alone. But I grew up in a family with four brothers and three sisters. Alone is something to cherish, a thing to hope for. I've arrived. Me, Phil Stone, alone on the second floor. Doing as I desire when I desire. Fresh out of college and on my first full time job. Paying rent, bills, and lugging my own groceries home.

Perhaps one day I'll desire human companionship, but not today. At least not tonight. It is so quiet I can hear the hot coals sizzle in the grill. The crickets outside singing their song of worship to the warm night sky.

Laura, my downstairs neighbor, had warned me, when we first met, about the dancing man. I was intrigued by her story. An older man who comes to the cemetery at least once a month and dances at the same gravestone.

"Is it the same dance every time?" I had asked her.

"I don't know," she answered. "I've never studied it that close. I just know about him. Everyone in the building does. It's kinda spooky, actually"

I notice Laura taking her garbage out. Making the walk across the back lawn to the dumpster. She is a short voluptuous woman. The same age as me, mid-twenties. A little round, but not overweight. Her baseball cap covers a majority of her blonde hair. She is dressed in house cleaning clothes. I recognized them because I remembered my Mother's cleaning clothes, worn jeans, a ratty looking t-shirt, dirty and smudged. This had to mean that she was off work for the day. Laura works from a home office doing case management for the elderly.

"You're the new guy in the building aren't you?" She had asked when we met. I was lucky to have only one bag of groceries then. We had run across each other in the hall and I was able to offer a handshake. She lived in the apartment directly below me.

"I am," I answered. "I've only been here a few weeks. I work during the day. "Her hands rested on her hips as she studied me." I work at the paper." She remained in her original position, hands on hips. Her demeanor gave no clue what I had said affected her one way or the other.

"Everyone has to do something," she had finally said.

I waved at her when she looked up at my balcony. The sun was disappearing over the horizon. Laura's round face and dimpled smile was barely visible in the increasing darkness. She noticed and waved back.

"Taking the night off?" she asked.

"Possibly," I answer. "Haven't committed one way or another."

"Need any help with that beer?" she asked, squinting to make sure I did have a bottle in my hand.

"Come on up," I offered. She walked toward the building. In a few seconds, she would be at my door.

Damn. I wasn't planning to work tonight, but I was going to enjoy the quiet. Still, Laura is very likeable. I popped the top off a bottle of cold beer while I waited for her knock on my door. When she did so, I met her with the open bottle. She took it and smiled.

"Thanks."

"Come in?" I asked. She followed me into the kitchen.

I grabbed my opened bottle and we toasted, smiling. "To nights off," I said. She took a drink. Let her gaze move around my apartment. This is the first time she had been inside my place. She raised the bottle as a gesture of acceptability. "Good beer," she said.

"Have you eaten?" I asked.

"I have," she said with a shy smile. "Smells good, I'm full though, go ahead. I'll just snoop around your living room."

My plate was set at the kitchenette bar. So I sat and started carving in. Laura walked about, studying pictures and magazines. My laptop was open and sitting at my small work desk, an unfinished game of solitaire still showing on the screen.

"Guess you are taking the night off," she observed.

Laura knew my story. I want to be a journalist. My boss had charged me with the assignment of writing a human-interest piece she might deem worthy of publication.

"Find me something about the human condition," my boss had ordered. Her name is Brigit and she seems to be one of those hard-nosed editor types. Like the kind portrayed on television. But in reality, she is probably just distracted. She usually has a look on her face like she is having trouble concentrating, most likely because she is thinking of something else other than the conversation at hand.

"Like a human accomplishment story?" I asked. Brigit just looked at me blankly. "A child prodigy maybe?"

"The human condition," Brigit repeated before turning her attention to some mundane piece of paper on her desk.

Tonight was two weeks since. In addition to the work I did at the office, I worked at home every night on the article. Usually in the presence of countless diet sodas and partially frozen TV dinners.

"Actually," I explained to Laura, "I'm finished with the project." I didn't really want to explain the whole story to her.

After hours of painstaking work, I had reported to Brigit's office with a story about a teenager who was about to win a scholarship for her musical ability. She was a child prodigy. A genius at the piano.

Brigit didn't read much of it before letting it fall to her desk. She turned her attention to something else in front of her and waved me off, without even looking my direction. As if she were the queen of England and she had suddenly become bored with me.

"I tire of you," the wave had said. "Be gone."

"Go or no go?" Laura asked, taking another swig from her beer.

"I was waved off," I told Laura.

"Waved off?"

"Literally."

"You got the wave?" Lester had asked. "Too bad," he said with a twinkle of humor in his eyes. Lester sits at the desk across from me. He is a seasoned reporter who had been working at the paper for a few years before my arrival. I suspected Brigit gave me the spot across from him on purpose. Maybe she always did with the new guys. Us kids who were still wet behind the ears, fresh from school. Hoping for a little of Lester to rub off on us.

Lester is not a bad sort, and he has no malice toward me. He never has a bad word to say about anyone. He delights in my efforts and delights even more in sending me for coffee. He said no more about the wave. I didn't ask. I never heard another word about it from Brigit. And the article was never published.

"Sorry," Laura said.

"It's okay," I said. "It's not like I was fired."

"Anything you can do about it?"

"Yup," I said, popping the top off another bottle. "I'm calling in sick tomorrow."

Laura raised her beer, as if toasting tomorrow. "I really love it here," she said. "Really like the quiet."

"You're alone down in your place?" I asked.

"Completely," she answered, handing me her empty bottle.

"I'll drink to that," I said, taking a swig from my fresh beer. Laura went home and I finished my steak.

The first thing I did in the morning was to get myself a cup of coffee, and picture Lester in the office fumbling with the coffee maker as he tried to remember how to do it himself. I turned on my laptop and opened the word processor. I typed the words "human interest". The words remained, luminous, while I spent the next few hours waking up and wandering the inside of my apartment, exploring and discovering my daytime home.

I prepared myself an egg sandwich and black coffee. It had been a long time since I played hooky. There was a mischievous joy to it I had not experienced since my childhood days. I drank down my last gulp of coffee out on the balcony. In the other room, the laptop powered itself down to standby mode. I looked out at the cemetery, and noticed a lone man.

The scene was puzzling, yet just as Laura had said. A tall dark man shuffling his feet apparently to some rhythm playing in his head. I could hear no music from my vantage point. He shuffled away in the middle of the cemetery, barely lifting his feet or moving his body. I made a decision to ignore him, and for a while it worked. I watched a little daytime television, went back to the laptop with nothing really in mind greater than a game of solitaire. On the way, walking by the balcony window, I saw him again, still out there shuffling his feet. By my clock, he had been doing so for nearly two hours. I was amazed, but still chose to ignore him. Perhaps he would go away. Perhaps I would never play hooky again. Perhaps the tall dark man dancing in the cemetery might never again disturb me.

Back at the computer I hit the power up key. The words "human interest" appeared on the screen. I sat in front of the laptop pondering this. "Disturbing," I thought to myself. I didn't like to be disturbed, anyone who knew me, knew this. My favorite movies are comedies, I only read magazines, and I never go to plays. I never want to be disturbed. The dancing man was disturbing. He was a story. But would he be waved away? I committed to the pursuit and put on my shoes.

He was still dancing when I arrived. The strange dance had been going on for close to three hours. The tall man was older looking up close. Maybe close to seventy. Sweat poured down his face. His eyes looked glazed over and distant. I had to fight the urge to call the hospital for an ambulance. The man didn't notice me. The sun was warm but there was a nice breeze, so the conditions were not extreme.

His feet moved in a hypnotic fashion, shuffling to and fro. I couldn't find a pattern for the longest time. I sat on a gravestone close by. He could see me if he wanted. Talk to me if he chose to acknowledge me. But he didn't. He just kept shuffling. I saw a pattern after a long while, a step he was doing. His arms barely moved, just his feet and legs, shuffling along, his knees slightly bent. One foot would shuffle, pigeon toed, in front of him across his path, in a wiggling type of movement. Then the other foot would do the same thing. Over and over, all the while his body moved in a half moon shape forward, and back again.

He was dressed casual. Like an older retired man out for an afternoon walk. Maybe out to get coffee and a bagel, a haircut, stop by the hardware store, say hi to the gang. Instead, he was here, dancing. His light pink button up shirt was soaked in a few places from his sweat. The cuffs of his dark pants were dusty from the dry ground. When the breeze kicked up a dust cloud would rise from the spot where his feet shuffled. His breath wasn't labored. He said nothing. He danced and never acknowledged me.

In front of him was a gravestone. The name on the stone was Miriam Sanders. She was born in May of 1927 and died the same month in 1997. The tall man never strayed from the marker. I considered he knew this woman, and was possibly married to her.

All at once he stopped, bowed to Miriam's stone and blew her a long and graceful kiss with both hands. As he turned to leave I asked him, "Are you okay?"

He looked at me in a funny way and answered, "Of course I am." He turned away from me to leave.

"If you don't mind?" I asked. "What was the dance you were doing? I've never seen anything like it before."

He stopped and turned to me. "You've never seen it because I made it up," he answered matter-of-factly.

"It's your dance?" I asked. He was walking away from me now and I had to walk quickly to keep up with the long legged man.

"I'm done now," he said over his shoulder.

"Done dancing?" I asked.

"Done dancing, and done with you."

"You can't come out to a cemetery like this and think no one will be curious about your dancing," I explained.

"Yes I can," he answered. We had arrived at his car which was parked along one of the many gravel roads crisscrossing the graveyard. My breathing became labored from trying to keep up with the man's swift stride. I reached for a pad and pencil, an action I immediately regretted.

"Do you mind if I ask you a few quick questions?" I asked.

"No you may not!" he answered with his eyes bulging out of his head from astonishment. He jumped into his car and drove off.

I would have followed him but my car was too far away. I walked dejectedly back to my apartment building. My pants caught and ripped as I climbed over the fence. Something I managed to avoid the first time over. When I arrived in the backyard of the building Laura was standing at the sliding glass door of her apartment.

"He won't talk to you," she announced to me.

"He did though."

"But he won't tell you anything."

"You've tried then?" I asked intrigued at her forwardness.

"I sure have," she answered. "So have other people I know of. He only says so much."

"How often does he do his dancing?"

"A couple times a month."

"Do you know any more about him?" I asked. "A name, anything?"

"I've climbed the fence also," she said. "I got the same information you did. I assumed he was married to the woman who is buried at the site he dances at. Eventually I stopped caring. He's very private."

"He told me he made up the dance himself."

"His name is Clyde," Laura informed me.

"Well that's pretty good," I complimented.

"It's a mystery," she added. "Have you considered he might be an escapee from some institution?"

"I'll try to find out for both of us."

Laura was willing to call me at work if he made another appearance. I walked back upstairs and sat in front of my laptop. I erased the words "human interest" from the computer screen and replaced them with the name "Clyde". I wrote very little after, but I got a start. Today was, after all, my day off.

"Interesting," Lester said the next day as he studied my notes. His head nodded up and down as he read, like he was agreeing with some great truth. "You should run this by Brigit."

"You think?"

"What's the worst that could happen?" Lester asked. "You get the wave again? With these notes you can get her to commit. Make her tell you up front."

"I'll take a few hundred words," Brigit said when she studies my notes. "Maybe a two part article."

"Really?" I asked.

She gave me a blank look as an answer. Of course "really". How silly of me. And Lester was right. She committed based on my notes. It was a done deal. I'd have to write a very poor article to be rejected again.

"My neighbor Laura is going to call me when she sees him dancing again," I informed Brigit. "I'll have to move fast when she calls."

"You might want to take Lester with you," Brigit suggested. "For backup."

When I close my eyes I could still see him doing the dance. The old man shuffling and swaying until reaching a trance state. There is a beauty to the dance. I think I recognized it from my balcony. The beauty is what intrigued me. Something astonishing was happening right under my nose. An otherworldly rhythmic motion, which perhaps had an origin from a force otherwise missing from my life. I close my eyes and I see him, all too often. Even when I am not expecting to, Clyde is there. It was a few weeks before I heard from Laura.

"Sure," Lester said, "I'll back you up. Cost you lunch and a mocha latte."

"Deal," I agreed. Seemed like a lot to pay for such a little bit of work. But it was ordained by the boss, and I was obliged to follow up.

We arrived together in separate cars at the cemetery. Standing next to my car, I could just make out Clyde across the grounds. A small cloud of dust was kicking up around him as he danced in the distance.

Lester and I approached Clyde. As Lester watched, an awkward expression formed on his face. He was either disturbed by Clyde or he was trying to recognize what he was doing. Clyde was in the middle of his dance and oblivious to us. His eyes had the familiar glaze to them I remembered from before. I could not tell, but Clyde seemed more tired. He was sweating and worn.

Lester bent to read the name on the gravestone. Then he stood and studied Clyde's feet. In a few minutes Lester was shuffling his feet in the same fashion as Clyde's. I felt a sudden wave of panic wash over me. This seemed like such odd behavior, especially for someone like Lester.

Within a few short minutes Lester had the movements down perfectly. Clyde never acknowledged him. The two of them kept shuffling and moving their bodies to some hidden rhythm I couldn't hear. This went on for another hour as I watched in the dry sun. Clyde suddenly stopped. He leaned over and blew a kiss to Miriam's gravestone. His eyes brightened with consciousness and he looked around. Lester was still dancing. Clyde noticed him and was not alarmed. He began to clap his hands in a slow rhythmic beat, keeping time for Lester. The dance continued with Lester not appearing to notice Clyde, and Clyde ignoring me. I didn't remove my notepad. I would remember this scene for the rest of my life. It was something I never expected. Lester danced for another half hour. His cell phone rang and he ignored it, or was unaware of it. My cell phone rang and I turned it off. He was sweating and his face was turning beet red. The wetness ran down his face and soaked his shirt.

Lester stopped, all at once, and began to cry softly. He turned to Clyde and bent to whisper in his ear. Clyde whispered something back. They carried on with this private exchange for a few moments, and then Lester turned to go. He looked at me as if he suddenly remembered I was there. He walked over to me and said, "It's called the Death Dance." That was all Lester ever said to me about it – ever. I watched him walk to his car and drive away. Later I found out he had called in sick for the rest of the day. I turned around and there was Clyde, still smiling.

Suddenly Clyde opened up to me. I assumed Lester had something to do with that, breaking the ice, making Clyde relax. I learned where he lived, he was eighty-five years old, and he was married to Miriam for fifty-three years. He lived on the bad side of town, which happens to old people often. The neighborhood was wonderful fifty years ago when they moved in. Over time the old neighborhoods go bad. The elderly with fixed incomes are trapped economically and rooted spiritually.

Miriam had died three years ago. Clyde was deeply in love with her all of his life, and still was. The two lived modestly in a three-bedroom home. They raised one child, Clyde Jr. who now lived out in California. Clyde Sr. had performed many various jobs before retirement. His list included janitor, security officer, car salesman, and insurance agent. He now lived on a modest pension supplemented by social security. I never learned of the Death Dance, except for what Clyde had already told me, he made it up.

"Did you have any luck?" I heard faintly as I breezed down the steps and out the back door of my building. It was the next morning and I was late for work. It took me a couple seconds to realize I had heard Laura's voice as I flew by. Opening the back door again, I found Laura standing there. Her hair down, white button up blouse, shorts which were not used for house cleaning, or any other chore except maybe shopping. Or to get someone to notice.

"Clyde?" I asked. She nodded her head. I told her about the experience Lester and I had.

"It would be interesting to know what he went through," she suggested. There was a longing in her eye. Something about Clyde, and now Lester, intrigued her.

"I'm late," I announced. "I wrote an article for my boss. We can discuss tonight if you like. Come up for a beer?"

"How about out for dinner?" she suggested. She was talking to her feet. Shy like. Afraid to meet my gaze. It must have been a lot for her to ask me.

"Absolutely," I said. Her eyes slowly rose to meet mine. Laura smiled. We didn't have dinner though. I'd received a call at work.

While fishing along the very stream we had fished so often in the past – attempting to lure a prize catfish onto his line, on a hot summer afternoon, not unlike those from my youth, a line in the water and the birds singing above – my father died.

The death of a parent will always bring out the true nature of the surviving siblings. My sister Iris and I joined to hire a lawyer for my mother's protection. In her distraught state she would have given away the entire estate to anyone who asked for it, and my brothers and sisters were asking, demanding actually, to my disgust, which I had little trouble displaying openly. We needed a quick court order just to keep a roof over our mother's head.

We worked with the lawyer, and I tried to keep my mind focused. These were no longer my brothers and sisters. These people were foreign to me. It was like I had never met them before. They cared not for my mother's needs, but continually cried about how deserving they were, with my father's dead body still warm in the grave. Except for my sister Iris, I went home never wanting to have contact with my family again.

For my father's funeral I had taken some acquired vacation time. A few of these days remained when I arrived home, and I took them. I soon found myself vegetating in front of the television. Laura knocked softly on my door holding a stack of bills and periodicals. She handed them to me silently, with a strange look in her eyes.

"I hope it wasn't too much trouble taking care of things," I said.

"It was okay. But something happened while you were gone."

"I didn't get evicted?" I asked sardonically while gesturing to the inside of the apartment with my arm.

"The article you wrote," she started.

"Yes?"

"It was printed while you were gone."

"Really?"

"You should go to the balcony."

I did, and looked out over the cemetery. A small crowd was gathered at Miriam's grave. Some people were dancing, some were watching. I had a hard time making them out so far away, but I was sure I didn't see Clyde.

"Phil," Laura said softly. She put her hand on my shoulder. "Clyde passed away when you went home to bury your father."

I was dumbfounded. Maybe because of all I had just been through, I could think of nothing to say. I saw Clyde's face in my memory. I could see into his wise eyes. I was empty inside.

"He was buried while you were gone," Laura said. "I'm so sorry." She took my hand in both of hers, looked up at me and smiled. She squeezed my hand and turned away. I knew she shared the sadness I was experiencing. Clyde was gone, and the secret of the dance with him.

I turned back to the balcony and closed my eyes. In my mind's eye I could see Clyde doing the death dance. Every step was etched into my memory. I took a deep breath, and I could see the sweat dripping from his dark chin. Concentrating on his feet, his face was bent to the task. The dust floated around him, kicked up by the shuffling of his feet. He was somewhere else then. He was somewhere the rest of us were not. Lester had been there, Clyde had shared it with him. The article, my father, Laura, all of the past weeks, along with the accompanying emotions, swirled within me.

I was disturbed. The dance called to me.

I climbed the fence and made my way to the grave. A crowd was gathered there, and I recognized none of them. I assumed they had all read the article I did not get to see in print. Some were dancing. Some watched. Some drummed softly on hand drums while toning melodies with their voices. The death dance was not to be successfully recreated by my readers.

Lester was nowhere in sight. Whatever he had received from the experience was his, and he wasn't going to share it.

"The dancer is dead," I said solemnly, to no one in particular. A fresh grave had been dug next to Miriam's resting place. I looked around at all of the curious faces. They knew something special had happened here, and hoped for someone to recreate it.

I closed my eyes and saw the old man. His face was weathered and worn. There was depth to it. Depth carved by time into the features of his face. I saw Clyde doing the death dance. Over and over again he shuffled his feet. Before I realized it, my feet were shuffling also, in the same fashion as the old man. I heard a low drum beat from the crowd. A heart beat rhythm matching the movements of my feet.

I continued the dance. I did it over and over, and over again. I continued until I was unaware of what I was doing. I danced until the dance took me over, as if it were an entity itself. As if it had a mind, a conscious, and a plan for me. The dance took over. It was the rhythm of a poem. The movements had the grace of the ages. It possessed me, and there was nothing else. There was no drumbeat, no people. There was no lawyer, job, car, apartment, and sunset, no Laura waiting to have dinner. There only existed the dance.

A dark and beautiful woman appeared to me. With my eyes closed, she showed herself to me in my mind's eye. In the sacred place at soul's depth, she appeared. A bright smile stretched across her face from ear to ear. She reached for me and I embraced her. I knew instantly she was Miriam. She was a happy woman, though with little reason. I could sense years of toil and strife. Years of carrying a burden she did not create. A burden of race and injustice.

"That's over now," I heard her say. Her voice was like music in my head. I thought if I were Clyde I would have created the death dance also, if only to hear the sweet music of Miriam's voice in my head.

He appeared to me then, Clyde, standing with his wife. He seemed unsure of himself. This was a new place for him. But he took comfort in being with Miriam, and she helped him. She knew the ways of this place. This universe I was now a part of. The world beyond death. Beyond the drumming and the dust from the shuffling of my feet. Clyde smiled at Miriam and held her hand. I smiled at the sight of them. Though he was uneasy now, I knew he would find happiness here with his beloved. Miriam turned her attention to me. She let go of Clyde's hand and walked to me. She reached a hand toward me and covered my eyes.

I was suddenly somewhere else. I was flying high above the ground. Below me the landscape passed by. Above was the clear blue sky with a few white lazy clouds floating on the air. I found I could control my movements, and I brought my flight closer to the ground. Gone were Clyde and Miriam. I was alone, and unaware of Miriam's hand over my eyes, if it was even still there. The landscape became familiar to me even though I had never seen it from this vantage before. The hills below me turned to a field of grass, then a small grove of trees. Through the grove a stream flowed, like fingers across a keyboard, like myself in a stream of consciousness. Ecstatic continuity. The reflection of my face in running water, mouthing to myself, "Disturbed."

This was my childhood home, and my father's before me. A small child stood at the bank of the stream with a fishing pole. He noticed me and waved, as if my flying over his head was the most natural of things to do. I easily brought myself down to stand beside him. He smiled at me and reeled in his line.

"Hello," he said to me. My father had spoken often of his childhood and I knew this to be the happiest place and the happiest time he could remember. He was an only child, and he fished the streams and hunted the woods.

"I'm sorry," the boy said to me.

"Don't be," I said.

"What about the others?"

"Thugs and thieves."

"I was afraid of that."

"It's under control."

"Are you taking care of your mother?"

"My sister Iris is."

He turned away toward the stream. I suspected he was crying. Iris. She was the strong one. She had the largest heart.

"I love you," he said to me.

"I know," I replied. "I love you too."

"Has this been rough?"

"As rough as these things can be."

"Listen," he said. He turned away and looked into the distance. He seemed to be looking at something far away I could not see. He turned back and looked me in the eye. It was a moment I will always remember. I could see pride in the young boy's eyes.

"You have to go now," he said. Miriam lifted her hand from my eyes. I saw her smiling face, a knowing look in her eyes.

"You're tired," she informed me.

She was right. I suddenly could feel exhaustion. My limbs were strained. As I thought about this I became more aware of myself and where I was. I was aware of my labored breathing, of sweat on my face and dust in my mouth.

"The dance," I thought to myself. I heard the drum beat in the distance. It was a wonderful chorus of rhythm. I knew it was the way home. Miriam and Clyde faded from my view.

I traveled back to the sound of the drummers. Resembling the tap tap tap of fingers on a typewriter, a sound I had not heard since my own childhood. My fingers on keys. The slide of the mechanism. The magic moment of ink penetrating paper.

I felt young again. A conquering hero returning from a journey of discovery. Learning how what I write could become real. What I danced created magic. I never would be alone. Iris would be there in the distance. Laura would hold my hand. Lester and I, sharing coffee. The boy fishing was forever proud, and a place would be waiting there next to him. A place familiar, where I could bask in the happiness of youth, and the constant flow. Continuity of life force.

My eyes opened and the crowd was still there. I turned toward the drumming, and saw Laura. She must have climbed the fence after me. Wonder filled her eyes. I was different, but in a familiar way. Like I was young again, I started walking on my weary legs and realized as I came nearer to Laura, I was becoming human again.

About the Author

IL Green's experience as a trained and certified mental illness specialist in the state of Illinois, and a person who suffers mental illness symptoms herself, has found a release of sorts in writing fiction. While writing is fun and adventurous, she still manages to include some of what she learned and experienced over the years successfully recovering from borderline personality disorder that often causes symptoms of depression and anxiety. She is an English major at Bradley University in Central Illinois and hopes to use her learned skills to enhance her writing ability. She currently occupies an empty nest in the same town as her university. Her degree is temporarily on hold as she cares for her elderly widower father and learns more about life, love, and loss than she ever considered possible.

Highlights of her history of publications include *Slice Magazine*, *Foliate Oak Online Literary Magazine*, *Downstate Story*, *Bluffs Literary Magazine* and *CaféLit*. Her novel *Girl of the Oil Sands* was released July 31st, 2022, via Outcast Press.

Like to Read More Work Like This?

Then sign up to our mailing list and download our free collection of short stories, *Magnetism*. Sign up now to receive this free e-book and also to find out about all of our new publications and offers.

Sign up here:
http://eepurl.com/gbpdVz

Please Leave a Review

Reviews are so important to writers. Please take the time to review this book. A couple of lines is fine.

Reviews help the book to become more visible to buyers. Retailers will promote books with multiple reviews.

This in turn helps us to sell more books… And then we can afford to publish more books like this one.

Leaving a review is very easy.

Go to https://bit.ly/3KuOx7S, scroll down the left-hand side of the Amazon page and click on the “Write a customer review” button.

Also by I.L. Green

Girl of the Oil Sands

Published by Outcast Press

Blades, babes, and the harsh beauty of love and nature. A begrudgingly heterosexual heroine often finds herself in nefarious situations as "a gal just trying to make a buck." Fueled by love, drugs, and delusion, Iris carries the weight of a dream in her heart as she treks from Florida all the way to Canada, ever in search of a home.

Befriended by another Hell-raiser in her 20s, Iris has her worldview and life path torn apart as if rearranged by her own machete. With her sexuality, resolve, and sanity called into question, Iris battles mental illness, ill-meaning men, and the icy wilderness. Disavowing a life of debauchery is hardly easy, but it's a war worth fighting.

Order from Amazon:

Paperback: ISBN 978-1737982-95-1
eBook: ASIN B0B6B264DH

Other Publications by Bridge House

I Knew it in the Bath

by Linda Flynn

I Knew it in the Bath is a collection of absorbing short stories which show that no matter how we expect events to unfold, life has a way of confounding us. What will a woman do to save her friend? Do we really know when we're being watched? Why did Dora throw the iron through the window? What's the best way to take revenge on a cheating partner?

Settle back for an engaging read through these humorous, sinister and thought-provoking stories, but try not to drop your book in the bath!

Linda Flynn, a frequent contributor to our annual themed anthologies, gives us food for thought in the stories collected in *I Knew in in the Bath.*

"I can't recommend this anthology enough. Linda Flynn has such a way with words." (*Amazon*)

Order from Amazon:

Paperback: ISBN 978-1-914199-28-8
eBook: ISBN 978-1-914199-29-5

Angels and Devils

by William Wilson

Cautionary tales of ordinary mortals doing extraordinary things.

From moral dilemmas to a Nativity miracle, the author takes us on a deeply thoughtful journey through eleven tales of the unexpected. Are the protagonists angels or devils, or even a bit of both? Would you help a friend to die? Would you tell your family if you inherited a fortune? Would you shelter a criminal from the law? We know these people and see their choices. What would we do in their place?

William Wilson makes us reflect in this collection of stories that take us by surprise.

"A great collection from William Wilson. The writer takes us into a number of diverse settings and times, with a real talent for creating character." (*Amazon*)

Order from Amazon:

Paperback: ISBN: 978-1-914199-24-0
eBook: 978-1-914199-25-7

The Sound of Patriarchy and Other Stories

by L.F. Roth

A collection of stories that runs the gamut from serious to comic. Relationships, and reactions to traumatic experiences or change, all come under scrutiny. Life-changing events play out against a counterpoint of minutely observed details.

Though you won't meet any bears in this volume, you will come across the real Dylan, delve into a literary feud, partake in preparations for a funeral rehearsal, share a musician's musings, find out the importance of gender-neutral watches and, perhaps, learn to stay clear of tigers, at least in the form of tattoos.

L.F. Roth brings us thought-provoking stories in *The Sound of Patriarchy and Other Stories*.

Order from Amazon:

Paperback: ISBN: 978-1-914199-26-4
eBook: 978-1-914199-27-1

www.ingramcontent.com/pod-product-compliance
Lightning Source LLC
LaVergne TN
LVHW010100110826
845155LV00028B/429